POUND

SAVING ABBIE BOOK 2

MAGGIE ALABASTER

Take Me Down Lower
    Written by Zeke Brantley

You make me feel so high,
    You make me feel myself.
    Touch me there so hard,
    Take me down lower.

You're all over me,
    Before I'm over you.
    Shove me to my knees,
    Take me down lower.

I can't stand,
    But I need to run.
    Cover me with thirst,
    Take me down lower.

Take me,
    Take me down lower.
    Take me,
    Take me down lower.

1

ABBIE

"EVIDENTLY SHE FOUND his head on her front doorstep in a cardboard box."

The words spun through my head over and over again like a song on repeat.

Somehow, I ended up sitting on the couch inside Zeke's inner-city Sydney townhouse, surrounded by the members of Wolf Venom, one of the hottest rock bands in the world. I didn't remember how I got there. At some point, I must have stepped inside. Everything was hazy but those words, spoken by a member of the press. Part of the pack which gathered outside on the sidewalk.

Someone pressed a cup of coffee into my hand. Judging by the smell, there was something harder in there than caffeine.

Fingers trembling, I put it to my lips for a sip. Yeah, there was a healthy dose of whiskey in there.

"Drink up, it will help to settle your nerves." That was Landon, his voice low and soothing. "Coffee and alcohol solve all problems."

I wasn't sure about that, but I took a big gulp anyway. It certainly took the edge off. The shock started to fade into acceptance. Vance was dead. Murdered. Left in a cardboard box, just like Jonah, the guy who pulled a gun on Zeke and I.

I was vaguely aware of Tully talking on the phone to someone.

"Jackson is on his way." The lead guitarist slipped his phone into his back pocket and sat in the chair opposite me. "Apparently Vance was found a couple of hours ago. Somebody leaked the story to the press. He's going to talk to them on your behalf and will deal with them. Jackson that is, not Vance." He managed a lopsided smile.

I nodded and gave him a watery smile in return for his attempt at humour.

"Thank you. I just..." I shook my head. "I can't believe it. I mean I hated him for what he did to me, but I didn't want him dead." Not exactly. "Who would do something like this? Why?"

Someone left Jonah's head in a box on Zeke's doorstep, and now this.

"This has to be aimed at me, doesn't it?" I looked around at the guys. "It can't be a coincidence."

Would the killer come after me next? My stomach churned and I regretted drinking the laced coffee.

"It'll be okay." Channing, the band's saxophone player, put an arm around me. He smelled of soap and a hint of something I couldn't put my finger on. A cologne maybe? Whatever it was, I liked it.

I leaned my head against his muscular chest and tried not to give in to uncontrollable trembling.

Under the circumstances, it was difficult. I kept imagining Vance's head looking back at me from inside a box. In my mind, his eyes were wide open, accusing me of somehow doing this to him.

Fuck off, I told my imagination. I had absolutely nothing to do with it. I hadn't seen him in person for over a year. Thank goodness I had plenty of alibis for the entire day. I was in the studio, recording a new album.

"What the hell is going on?" Asher's voice made me jump so hard I almost spilled what was left of my coffee.

He and Zeke stepped in through the back door,

identical expressions of confusion and worry etched on their gorgeous faces.

"We saw the circus out the front so we had to come around the back way." Zeke crouched down in front of me and placed his hands lightly on my knees.

"Are you okay?" he asked, his voice rough with worry.

"Yeah," I said. "Vance is dead."

He blinked in surprise, then set his mouth in a hard line. "The asshole who married you as a publicity stunt? I'm not sure if I can be persuaded to give a shit. Sounds like good riddance to me." He was uncompromising when it came to people he cared about.

People like me. I could hardly believe how close I got to him and the other guys in such a short time. Already, they meant more to me than anyone else ever had. It was becoming more and more evident the feeling was mutual all around.

"Yeah, I guess," I said. "But he was found the same way Jonah was. Just his head in a cardboard box." I swallowed to keep from throwing up. No one deserved to end up like that, no matter how shitty they were.

I didn't want to, but had to ask. "Where were you

and Asher?" Did I even want the answer to that? They could have been up to something shady I was better off not knowing about.

Zeke looked surprised, then laughed, just slightly. "Not killing Vance. I can promise you. I wish I thought of it, but I didn't do it."

I wasn't sure if he was joking or not. He actually looked like he'd give the killer a high five for their trouble. That was both hot and oh-so-wrong at the same time.

I looked over at Asher. The drummer shook his head, but he too looked like he wished he was in on it.

He raised his hand. "I solemnly swear we didn't kill him."

"I believe you," I said. I really did.

Asher and Zeke exchanged glances.

"She might feel better if she knew where we were," Asher said reluctantly.

Zeke shrugged, then nodded. "I guess so." He sighed through his nose and said, "We went to see Reuben, to tell him to leave you the fuck alone."

Zeke's brother was a lot older, and the head of his family. Not just family of relatives, but criminal activity too. Mobsters, mafia, whatever you wanted to call them. Reuben was adamant Zeke would quit the band and return to the family someday. Zeke was adamant he wouldn't. Reuben tried to recruit me to convince Zeke, but that hadn't gone down very well. With me or Zeke.

"Let me guess, he didn't like that," I said. "You don't think he had anything to do with what happened to Vance, do you?"

Zeke was certain Reuben wasn't behind killing Jonah, because Jonah worked for Reuben. That didn't mean he wasn't behind Vance's death.

Zeke frowned. "It's his style, but I don't know why he would have Vance killed."

"So I would be put back under scrutiny," I suggested. "This could have a really negative impact on the tour." As in, make everything ugly as shit.

In only a couple of weeks, I was supposed to leave with Wolf Venom to tour the world. It was supposed to resurrect my career and reputation after my very brief marriage and very public affair with the owner of my former label, Onyx Riot Records.

"I might get kicked off the tour." Tears prickled in the corners of my eyes. "The label might cancel my new album."

If that was the case, I was done for. My career would be over once and for all. I would be lucky to get a job waiting tables. It was so unfair. I hadn't worked this hard just to have it all come crashing down on me for something I had nothing to do with.

Zeke put an arm around me, so I was held between him and Channing, drawing warmth and comfort from them both. "No one is kicking you off the tour. Or cancelling the album. I promise. I'm not going to let that happen to you. Or to us, because the band needs you along on this tour."

"That's debatable."

I hadn't realised Penn arrived until he spoke. Now, he stood a couple of metres away, his arms crossed over his chest, his usual pissed off expression on his face.

"What the fuck is going on?" he asked. "Jackson called and told me to get here as quickly as possible. You're all moping around here like you're at a funeral. Who died?"

"Hey Penny," Asher greeted. "Abbie's ex-husband died."

Penn's scowl deepened. "Who gives a shit?"

"He was murdered," Tully said.

Penn shook his head. "I still don't care."

"The same way Jonah was," Zeke said. "As in, there might be a serial killer running around Sydney. You might be next."

Penn dropped his arms. "Okay, *now* I care." He

looked at me through narrowed eyes. "This has something to do with you? I told you guys she was trouble. Did you believe me? No. You're all too busy thinking with your cocks."

"Right, and you're not?" Asher said.

"What's that supposed to mean?" Penn demanded.

The conversation was interrupted by a knock on the door.

Asher peered through the window, toward the street. "It's Jackson." He opened the door to let the manager in, and closed it quickly before any of the press could push their way inside.

Jackson looked frazzled. Landon handed him a coffee. He gratefully took a sip.

"Abbie, I've spoken to the police and told them you were in the studio all day. They said they wanted to confirm a few things. No one thinks you had anything to do with this."

I sighed gratefully. "I hope not. It's still not a good look though, is it?" I grimaced tentatively.

He looked like he wanted to deny it, but regretfully said, "No, it's not. The timing isn't the best either. We'll make it clear you know nothing about what happened and feel terrible about him dying. We'll put together a statement for the press. They will have to be satisfied with that. Otherwise, we'll be keeping all of you under wraps until this blows over."

"How long will that take?" Penn looked at me as though this was all my fault.

Was he right? If someone was targeting me, was it fair for them to have gotten caught up in all of this too? I didn't think so, but I was grateful I wasn't alone in all of this. That was selfish of me, I knew, but it was what it was.

"You know what the press is like," Jackson said wearily. "They'll move on to something else in a day or so."

"Or Wolf Venom could distance ourselves from her right now," Penn suggested.

"Fuck off," Asher told him. "First of all, she is one of us now, whether you like it or not. Secondly the press would crucify her if we did that and you know it. She doesn't deserve that." He gave Penn a scathing look like perhaps he did.

Penn glared at him. He slumped back against the wall and crossed his arms over his chest again. It seemed he'd said his piece and was now going to see how it all unfolded.

I gave Asher a grateful smile. I didn't want the band to be at odds with each other over me, but his growling at Penn was kinda hot.

Zeke gave him a look that suggested he found it just as hot. If those two guys weren't careful, they were going to set me on fire.

I was totally here for it.

"No one is distancing themselves from anyone," Jackson said firmly. "I've spoken to Levi Jones and he agrees. If anyone is to ask, and they will, Wolf Venom is one hundred percent behind Abbie Hart. White Wolf Records is one hundred percent supportive as well. However, Levi is also glad Abbie has an airtight alibi."

"Me too," I agreed wholeheartedly. Any other day and I would have been just about anywhere in Sydney, doing fuck knows what. If anyone was trying to pin this on me, they screwed up.

I was totally here for that too. The sooner they found whoever did this, the better.

To Zeke, I said, "Do you think we slowed the police down by disposing of Jonah's head?"

He scrubbed his cheek with his hand. "No way to know. We can't undo it now. If we let the cops know we found it, we'll only get ourselves into trouble." He threw his hand up in frustration. "I wish we knew about it before the press did. We could have made it all go away by now."

"Do I want to know how?" I asked.

He grinned. "No, you don't. I'll just say I know people and leave it at that."

"I'm going to pretend I didn't hear that," Jackson said.

Zeke pointed a finger gun at him. "Good idea. You don't want to know about it either."

"I very much don't," Jackson agreed. "Everything you said needs to stay within these walls. We're all complicit if it doesn't. You don't need me to tell you what that would do to your careers." His eyes lingered on Penn in particular.

"We'd be fucked," Penn said. "That's what it would do."

His words were a relief. I half expected him to say he was going to talk to the press and throw me under the bus. Anything to get rid of me.

"Exactly." Jackson swallowed down the last of his coffee. "We've all worked too hard to throw it away now." He handed his cup to Channing. "I need to go and put out some more spot fires. Preferably before it turns into a full-blown bushfire. Stay away from the press. Either stay here or go to your homes and lock the doors. Don't answer phones. Consider this a gag order from the boss. If they have any questions, they can go through me and our lawyers."

Asher unlocked the door and let Jackson back

out into the insanity of the throng outside. He quickly locked it again. "Isn't this exciting?"

"I could use a bit less excitement," I said. "Or at least a different kind of excitement."

Asher grinned.

2

ASHER

"It's going to be a tight fit," Zeke said.

I grinned.

He rolled his eyes at me. "Dude, I wasn't talking about that."

"Sure you weren't, dude." I was. It felt like I waited a lifetime for him and Abbie.

What I wanted, more than anything, was to be transparent with them. I needed to be with both of them, in every way that mattered, but I didn't want to sneak around to do it. I wanted everyone to know who was doing what with who, and for us all to be cool with it. Otherwise, we'd fuck up what we had before it began.

"Landon and Channing can sleep in my spare room," Zeke continued, one eye on me. "Tully and

Penn can crash on the couches downstairs. That leaves you, me and Abbie to squash up in my bed."

"I bags being in the middle," I said quickly. I eyed the door to the bathroom. The shower was still running. "Do you think she's okay in there?"

Zeke glanced towards the door, a frown on his brow. "Yeah. Give her a couple of minutes more. If she doesn't get out, I'll go and check on her." He opened his wardrobe and pulled out a spare pillow.

"And by check on her, you mean offer to wash her back?" I teased.

He smiled and tossed the pillow onto the bed. "If I don't, someone else will."

"You're right," I agreed. "I would absolutely offer. Since I'm a nice guy, I would offer to wash your back too. In fact, I have two hands. One for each back."

"I think you might be overestimating the size of my shower," he said dryly.

"I think it might be time to move then." The size of the shower was definitely a reason to sell a property, right? I watched enough of those home renovation shows to know party showers were a thing. We were rock stars, we had no excuse *not* to have a party shower in each of our homes.

Although, we were also new to the concept of sharing in the way we were talking about now.

"I'll think about it." Zeke pulled a pillowcase out from a drawer and started to put it on the pillow. "I could buy the place next door and blow out the walls between that and this. I could have a couple of big bathrooms and four bedrooms."

"There's that word again," I said with a happy sigh. "Blow."

He looked over at me and grinned. "It's one of my favourite words."

"Me too." I gave him a long, lingering look. He and I had been friends since we were kids, but this whole flirtation thing was new. I liked it.

My heart was in my throat, because I didn't want overstep and screw this up, I put a hand on Zeke's muscular-as-fuck bicep and gave him a light kiss on the mouth.

I thought he might stiffen in discomfort or even push me away. But like the other night, he kissed me back with an equal amount of intensity, and a little bit of tongue.

I moaned against his mouth, enjoying the way his stubble tickled my lips.

He must have dropped the pillow, because his hands were on my hips and his body was pressed up against mine. Careful not to bump my erection on his, I slid my arms around his neck.

"Holy shit." Abbie's soft voice came from the doorway.

I started to break off the kiss.

"Don't stop on my account," she said. "I'm more than happy to watch."

Fuck, that was hot.

"We'd prefer it if you joined us," I said. "Wouldn't we, Zeke?"

His face was pink and his lips were parted like he was trying to catch a breath.

"Yeah," he agreed. "But I have to get these pillows down to the guys before they bitch about not having any. Save some for me."

He grabbed the pillow and another one he'd already put the cover on and carried them to the door. He stopped to give Abbie a deep, lingering kiss on the way past.

She looked adorable in a white fluffy dressing gown and a towel wrapped around her hair. Her skin was red from the heat of the water but with no makeup on, she looked even more gorgeous than ever.

She stepped into the room and closed the door behind her. She unwound the towel from her head and let it fall to the floor. Her blond hair tumbled loose to her shoulders.

"Do you want me to brush it?" I offered. Anything to touch her.

"Sure." She crouched and pulled a hairbrush out from the soap bag inside an open suitcase on the floor. Apparently she hadn't finished unpacking it.

I knew this living arrangement was supposed to be temporary, but Zeke would happily let her stay forever.

"Sit down on the bed," I said when she stood and hesitated. "Are you feeling a bit better now?" I took the brush and started to run it gently through her hair. Every so often, I stopped to tease out a tangle. If it hurt, she gave no sign. If anything, she seemed to be enjoying the attention.

"A little bit," she agreed. "Alcohol and a hot shower solve most problems, don't they?"

"Only the ones that can't be solved with sex," I agreed.

"I dunno, sometimes I think sex creates more problems than it solves," she said with undisguised bitterness.

"Only if you're having sex with the wrong people." I finished one side of her hair and started on the other. "The right people make all the difference."

Like the rest of the guys, I had my share of partners. Mostly one night hook ups. I worried I might never be interested in anything longer lasting than that. Now, it all made sense. I was waiting for Zeke and Abbie.

Did they feel the same way? I hoped like hell they did.

"There you go, perfect." I placed the hairbrush on Zeke's chest of drawers and bent to kiss her head. Of course, now I'd do what I could to mess her hair up again.

"Thank you." She looked over her shoulder at me, her blue eyes full of promise.

"You're welcome." I slid my hands down either side of her face, down her neck. I brushed her throat with my fingers and let them dance over her skin, down the front of her dressing gown. I lightly massaged every centimetre of her, all the way down to the softness of her full breasts.

I had waited approximately a lifetime to touch her like this. Potentially several lifetimes.

"Mmm," she breathed when I ghosted the heels of my palms over her nipples. They hardened eagerly under my touch. I pinched each one between my thumb and forefinger and rolled them, savouring the way her breath hitched in response.

"Nipples are one of my favourite things." I made

myself a bet that I wouldn't find any part of her I didn't want to touch over and over again.

She undid the belt on her dressing gown and let it slide down over her shoulders and off her arms. Her skin was pale except for freckles scattered here and there.

"Wow, you're gorgeous." I bent to brush my lips over her shoulder, then moved around to sit beside her, facing her.

"No, you." She wound her arms around my neck and drew me in for a searing, hot kiss. The kind that would make me see stars for days. She tugged up the hem of my T-shirt and somehow managed to get it off without breaking our lips apart for more than a second or two.

She leaned back. Her eyes raked over me.

"See, this is what I mean. You guys are like… Holy hotness. How are any of you even real?"

"Maybe we're not— Oh!" She took me by surprise when she put her hands on my chest and shoved me back onto the mattress. I wasn't complaining. No way.

I certainly wasn't complaining when she shed the rest of the dressing gown and slowly crawled up my body. She straddled my hips and lowered her mouth to mine.

The offensive fabric of my pants was the only thing between us. Everything felt too tight, like my cock was ready to break the seams to get to her. I wanted to hurry up and get out of them, but at the same time I wanted to slow down and not rush.

In the end, she was the one who undid the button and slowly worked the zipper down, as the door opened and closed. The lock clicked into place.

A moment later, Zeke was next to us, already without his shirt.

Thank you universe.

"Looks like I got back just in time," Zeke said.

"We would have waited." Although, when she grabbed the sides of my pants and slid them down my hips, then curled her hand around my erection, I realised that might have been hard. Um, difficult.

"Sure you would." Zeke's eyes were on my cock. They widened when Abbie moved down and started to run her tongue over my tip.

I reminded myself this was new to him. I had to take it slow and not scare him off.

I locked my eyes on him and placed a hand on his shoulder. Gently, giving him time to resist and move away if he wanted to, I drew him towards me. At first, it was just a light brush of lips against lips.

He lifted himself up on his elbow and deepened the kiss.

The touch of both of them was everything I hoped for and more.

I slipped my tongue inside Zeke's mouth as Abbie lowered hers over my cock and started to suck.

I groaned with the pure pleasure that pulsed all the way through me.

Slowly and carefully, I slipped my hand down to work the button on Zeke's pants loose. He lifted his hips and between us we pushed his pants down. He kicked them off the rest of the way.

"If any of this is uncomfortable, just tell me and I'll stop," I told him.

"You know it, bro," he said.

I wasn't sure if *bro* was the right word under the circumstances, but I would roll with it.

My eyes on his, I closed my fingers around his cock.

His eyes half closed and he tensed just a little bit, but he didn't pull away.

Encouraged, I started to run my hand slowly up and down his length. It didn't take long for his hips to move in rhythm with me. It was so insanely hot, I could barely handle it.

"Abbie," I managed to say over the pounding blood in my brain. "I want to be inside you. Please."

She picked up her head, gave my cock a couple more teasing swipes with her tongue, then crawled up the bed to me.

I let go of Zeke, rolled her onto her back and knelt between her legs. I took a moment to admire the view of her open thighs and already glistening pussy. Slowly at first, I explored her folds and clit with the tips of my fingers, before slipping a couple inside her to make sure she was ready for me.

"She's practically dripping," I said to Zeke.

He flashed a grin while he worked his hand up and down his cock. A bead of moisture formed on his tip, making my balls heavier than ever. I needed to touch him. I needed to bury myself in her. I needed everything, all at once.

I positioned my cock carefully outside Abbie's warm, damp pussy and slowly slid inside her glorious body.

The groan she gave was almost enough to make me come on the spot. Holy hell, she felt incredible. Even more than I could have imagined.

I reclaimed Zeke's cock, curling my hand back around him while leaning on my opposite elbow.

He lay on his side and kissed Abbie while I thrust

into her and worked him at the same time. It took some concentration to get the rhythm right, especially when I was distracted by the way his hand slid over her breasts. His fingers swirled over her skin, teasing her nipples while he became more and more breathless.

He slid his hand down, over her belly and between her thighs. He must have found her clit, because he started to rub, fingers tracing circles over her. She arched her back and moaned.

Every time I thrust, I felt his calloused skin, and the crazy amazing heat of her core.

My hand tightened around his cock. I didn't know whose breathing was more ragged at this point. Maybe it was a three-way tie.

I pounded harder and harder and worked him faster and faster.

Abbie moaned loudly. "I'm going to come," she said.

"Me too," I said breathlessly.

Her eyes flickered open. "Asher... Come inside me."

Oh... Fuck. When she put it that way...

She came first, crying out. Her back arched harder and her muscles tightened around me.

I was next, a moment later, grinding hard for

every drop of pleasure. For a long, wonderful moment nothing existed but orgasms and a burst of rainbow in my vision.

Zeke came shortly after, thrusting into my hand, and spilling warm, pearly cum over my fingers.

I gave a long low grunt and finally sagged, my hand curled tight around the most gorgeous man, cock still inside the most beautiful woman I ever saw.

I thought I was living before this, but now I knew I just started.

3

ABBIE

THE FIRST THING I felt when I woke up was warmth.

I was tucked in tight between two rock hard bodies. Zeke on my left and Asher on my right. Zeke lay facing me, one arm lying over my stomach. Asher was lying on his back, one of his legs draped over one of mine.

There were worse ways to wake up than between two hot rock stars. Particularly when both of them seemed to care about me as much as I cared about them.

Zeke and I hadn't talked about his feelings since he told me he was falling for me. I sensed his hadn't changed. Mine grew the more I got to know all of the guys.

I wanted to punch Penn in the dick more often

than not, but he was ridiculously hot and talented. The seven of us were becoming so embedded in each other's lives that it was hard not to include him when I thought about the collective *us*.

He might disagree, possibly strenuously, but that was how I felt.

I gradually became aware that Zeke was awake and watching me.

"Hey," he said softly.

"Good morning." I had a sneaking suspicion it was closer to afternoon than morning but whatever. Shit like that doesn't matter when you're in the middle of two guys like this. "Did you sleep well?"

"I always do when you're next to me." He pressed a kiss to my nose.

"And Asher?" I was worried Zeke might freak out about kissing and touching another guy. It was one thing to get caught up in the moment and another to have to deal with that moment afterwards.

"Him too," Zeke said after a moment. "You're not weird about this?"

"No," I said quickly. "You're the one who told me all the guys in the band wanted to do, what was it, naughty things to me? It seems like you were right."

He smiled. "Of course I was. I know the guys. For

good or not so good, depending on your perspective."

I laughed softly. "It must be hard spending so much time together. Work and play and everything in between."

"It certainly is hard." He grabbed my hand and drew it down to his erect cock.

"So it is." I stroked my hand up and down his length and toyed with his balls for a minute or two.

At the same time, he reached down between my thighs and started to circle my pussy with his fingertips. He carefully stayed away from my clit until he'd touched every other part of me, including sliding his fingers through my folds and over my rear hole.

When he finally touched my clit, I was already panting.

"Are you two starting without me?" Asher asked sleepily. Apparently he woke quickly, because a moment later he was swirling his tongue around my nipple and starting to suck.

"We're just getting started," I said, breathless already.

"Oh good," Asher said around a mouthful of nipple.

Zeke slipped a couple of fingers inside me and

hooked them around to massage my G spot. He leaned over and licked my other nipple.

All that attention on the three most sensitive parts of my body drove me towards the edge faster than a runaway train.

I kept my eyes half open and watched them work on me, while trying to get my head around how incredible it was to be here with both of them. A girl could definitely get used to this.

I wanted to hold on for longer, but I toppled over the cliff and into an intense orgasm that thrummed through my entire body like an electric guitar with the volume turned up to full. I cried out or maybe I screamed. All I really knew was that every bit of me was on fire in the best way possible.

I flopped, panting, onto the mattress. My head went on spinning for a minute or two.

When it was finally clear, I looked from one guy to the other.

"What?" Zeke asked. He gave me that look like he was sure I was up to something, but didn't know what.

I rolled over just far enough to open the drawer beside the bed.

"Oh." Zeke swallowed audibly.

Asher's eyes widened when I pulled out the

vibrator and tube of lube. "Okay, this just got interesting."

"It wasn't interesting before?" Zeke asked. He took the vibrator and lube from me and, after a moment's pause, handed it to Asher.

"It was, but this is even more so." Asher opened the tube and applied the lube to the vibrator while Zeke rolled me onto my back and knelt between my knees.

He slowly slid his cock inside me, his eyes half closed. They closed fully and he gulped again when Asher sat beside him and held the vibrator near his ass.

"You've done this before?" Asher asked.

"Once," Zeke said, his voice strained. "Be gentle."

"Of course," Asher said lightly. "Let me know if you want me to stop."

I, for one, was glad Zeke and I played with the vibrator before. I had a feeling he wasn't quite ready to have Asher's cock in his ass or mouth. Or to have Asher suck him.

Someday, but not yet.

Zeke jerked a little, but then he let out a huffing moan that sounded like he was enjoying the way everything felt.

As much as I loved being the centre of attention

for both guys, I liked that Zeke was in the centre now. Everyone deserved to feel special.

I couldn't help but wonder what the press outside would think if they knew what was going on inside the townhouse. I'd be happy if they never knew, but I wasn't ashamed of anything we were doing either.

I mean, I wasn't going to let anyone film us and put it on the internet, but I wasn't going to be embarrassed either. I've done plenty of embarrassing things in my life; having sex with two guys wasn't one of them.

"Is that okay?" Asher asked.

"Mmm-hmm," Zeke said in reply.

Of course he couldn't respond with coherent words. It was hard enough to think with his cock inside me, much less being stimulated from two angles.

Gradually, Zeke started to move, sliding out of me, then slipping slowly back in. From the look of concentration on his face, he was trying to get a rhythm of thrusts that Asher could match.

"I knew you two would be amazing," Asher said. "I didn't realise you would be *this* amazing."

"We should both come with a warning label," I managed to say.

Both guys chuckled.

"Accurate," Asher said. His voice was strained. He seemed to be very much enjoying what he was doing, but I didn't need to look to see he was also hard.

"Would you like some help?" I offered.

"Zeke?" Asher asked.

"It's okay," Zeke managed to say. "Don't want you to pop anything."

Asher chuckled. "In that case, yes please." He slipped the vibrator free, put it aside and scooted up the bed until his groin was in front of my face. I tipped my head, opened my mouth and let him slide his cock between my lips.

Almost as though they played together for so long they knew each other's rhythm, the guys started to pump into me in unison.

Filled with Zeke's cock, and with the taste of Asher on my tongue, I flowed effortlessly toward another orgasm, this one softer, but somehow more mind blowing than the first one.

I definitely screamed this time, but cut off the sound as Asher came. I clamped my lips around him as he pounded harder, grunting and grinding until hot cum spilled into my mouth.

I took a breath through my nose and swallowed as Zeke came, pounding just as hard into my pussy.

The whole world disappeared in a whirlpool of heat and sweat, grunts and moans. The slide of hot male skin on mine, tattoos and calloused hands. I could happily have stayed in this place for eternity.

We all slumped back down with sighs and pants. I was so slick with sweat by now, I was going to need another shower.

"Do we have to go on tour?" Asher asked. "Can't we stay here in bed instead?"

"Believe it or not, other places in the world have beds," Zeke said. "And get this, you don't always need a bed."

"What?" Asher said jokingly. "Are you trying to say there are other places which are perfectly acceptable for fucking?"

"I am saying that," Zeke said. "Lots of them. I'm pretty sure the three of us can find quite a few, if we put our minds to it."

"You guys," I said teasingly. "I'm certain you're both creative when it comes to finding a place."

I've been on tour enough times to know there were all sorts of nooks and crannies, even if you have to look for them, and rarely a shortage of someone happy to share them with you.

"Like a dark corner in a nightclub?" Zeke smiled slowly.

"Exactly," I agreed.

"You what now?" Asher asked.

I turned my head and watched his expression as Zeke told him how he and I met.

"Dude, where was I when this was going on?" Asher asked.

"I think you were suffering through dinner with Dane," Zeke said.

"I knew I should have missed it," Asher groaned. "For so many reasons, including that."

I rolled over and kissed his mouth. My lips were probably still red from his cock. "We'll make it up to you."

He kissed me back and then pressed his nose against mine. "You already have. Twice already. That isn't to say I'm not up for many, many more."

"I had a feeling you might be," I said.

"Can we pack the vibrator?" Asher asked Zeke.

"I would be disappointed if you didn't," Zeke replied. "As long as I get to use it on you two, too. Actually, I have a few different types in the drawer. We could take them all and play around."

"We could use one to find out what's up Penny's ass," Asher said jokingly.

"His head," I said dryly. It was either that or a stick. Whatever it was, I wished he would take it out and lighten up. Or at least stop being an asshole to me.

They both laughed.

"That makes sense," Zeke agreed. He sighed. "I suppose we should get up and see if the press is still camped out the front, waiting for blood."

I didn't want to move, but I needed to know if they were still out there too. Shit.

Could I put the blankets over my head and hide for another year or ten instead?

4

ABBIE

THE PRESS WERE outside the townhouse all morning but slithered away by lunchtime. No doubt they were off making someone else's life miserable.

"Just in time," Zeke said cheerfully.

"Yeah," Penn said. "We were just about to kill each other."

Apart from having to share the bathroom, all the guys got along pretty well. In spite of what the keyboard player said, no one seemed ready to murder anyone else.

"No we weren't," Zeke said. "We are going on a little excursion. The bus will be outside shortly."

Penn narrowed his eyes at him. "The fuck? Where are we going?"

"Trust me," Zeke said lightly. "You'll love it."

Penn muttered and stalked off towards the kitchen. He didn't say he wouldn't go.

That seemed pretty miraculous to me. He didn't seem like the kind of guy who liked excursions very much.

On the other hand, Zeke's idea of an excursion might be to a strip club for all I knew. Although, if that was the case, we would just all walk.

"Any idea what's going on?" I asked Asher, who sat beside me on the couch eating toast.

"No idea," Asher said. "Whatever it is, it's bound to be good. Every once in a while Zeke organises shit like this. It's always pretty sick."

"We're not going to jump out of a plane are we?" I grimaced around the lip of my coffee cup. I was game for just about everything, but that was not high on my to-do list.

Asher glanced towards the window. "I doubt it. It looks too windy out there for that. Might rain too. My guess is that it's an indoor activity." He wiggled his brows at me. "My favourite kind."

I smiled back. "Mine too."

"No shit," Penn grumbled. "You three were loud enough."

"Sorry, not sorry," Asher said without taking his eyes off me.

"I hope it's the trampoline place again," Landon said. "That was fun."

"My guess is paintball or laser tag," Channing said. He looked like he relished the idea of shooting his bandmates. With paint.

"We could be going to a movie," Tully suggested. "My guess is a private screening of the latest super-hero movie."

"I could get behind that," Penn said. "Put me down for a super-sized tub of popcorn."

"I'm going to guess go-kart racing," Asher said.

"Any of that would be better than jumping out of a plane." Personally, I liked the idea of curling up in front of a movie screen. Including the popcorn. That might be the first time I agreed with anything Penn said. That was another miracle right there.

"Anything would be better than jumping out of a fucking plane again," Penn said. He gave Zeke a death stare.

Zeke shrugged unapologetically. "You didn't have to jump. For the record, you're all wrong, but if somebody wants to write all those things down, I'll plan them for another time."

"Landon," Channing said to him.

"On it." Landon pulled out his phone and started

tapping at the screen. "I'm going to add bungee jumping to the list."

"Don't you fucking dare," Penn growled.

"You don't have to jump," Zeke said patiently, like he was talking to a child.

"I'm not going to get there and then not jump," Penn argued. "But I don't want to get there in the first place."

Once again, I found myself agreeing with him. I would also do it if I was there and they were egging me on, but the idea was terrifying. If I wanted a shot of adrenaline, I would get up on stage, or crawl under a table in a nightclub and suck one of the guys off. For the most part, neither of those would kill me.

"Maybe Penny would prefer a visit to the museum," Asher said.

Penn flipped him off.

"I like museums," I said.

"I'll add that to the list," Landon said.

Penn gave me a look like I wasn't going to be around long enough to go on any excursions to the museum with the band.

I was determined to prove him wrong. He didn't have to like me. Whatever his opinion was, that was his problem, not mine. While I was hanging out with the rest of the band, he would have to put up with me. It would be nice if he would shut up as well, but he was who he was.

"The bus is here," Zeke said. "Everyone on board, boys and girls." He opened the door and peered outside. "If any of the press are still lurking around, I can't see them."

We all piled cups and plates into the kitchen sink and stepped outside into the sunshine.

The bus was small, the kind designed to fit about fifteen to twenty people comfortably. I had half hoped it was one of those big tour buses with a king-size bed at the back, but it was still exciting to be going somewhere interesting with the band.

"Where are we going?" Asher asked the driver as he led me onto the bus, my hand in his.

"Good try," Zeke said as he put his hand on my ass and pushed me up the steps. "She's not gonna tell you anything."

"Nope," the driver agreed. Her head was shaved except for a millimetre or two of hair, and she had more piercings than I'd ever seen on one person. She also had the kind of huge smile that made me like her immediately.

"I got paid extra to keep my mouth shut."

"Ren has worked for the label for a long time,"

Zeke explained. "She drives the tour bus and helps set up the stage."

Ren snorted. "Helps, my ass. I do most of the heavy lifting the boys can't handle."

"She's not joking," Asher said. "She's a certified badass."

"Shit yeah, I am," Ren agreed. She gave me a warm smile. "It's nice to meet you. Word to the wise though. At least half of the stuff that comes out of these guys' mouths is bullshit."

"Hey," Asher protested. "We're not that bad."

I grinned back at Ren and let the guys herd me to the back seat of the bus. It was the only place where three people could sit next to each other. I sat in the middle with Zeke on one side and Asher on the other.

Channing and Landon sat together in front of us. Tully sat on the opposite side of them.

Penn sat by himself at the front of the bus, sideways with his feet on the seat. He pulled out his phone and started to tap on the screen, the usual scowl on his face the entire time.

"So we're not allowed to know where we're going," I said slowly. "Are we allowed to know how long it will take us to get there?"

"That depends on traffic," Zeke said.

"This is Sydney, everything depends on the traffic," Asher pointed out.

"I should have asked, on a good day how long will it take us to get there?" I clicked my seatbelt into place.

"On a good day, maybe fifteen minutes," Zeke said. "But because this is Sydney, probably three hours." He grinned.

I snorted softly. Even on a bad day, it wasn't usually that bad. Unless a vehicle broke down on the Harbour Bridge or something. Then three hours might be a conservative estimate.

"With Ren's driving, we'll get there in ten minutes," Asher said. As if to keep me from falling off the seat in case of an emergency, he placed his hand on my thigh.

Zeke did the same to my other leg.

I felt much safer now if an accident occurred. And I hadn't seen any sign of the press.

Bonus.

The police stopped by shortly after we got out of bed, but they had little to say, or ask. They'd already been to the studio and clarified my whereabouts that day. According to them, I wasn't considered a suspect.

No doubt they'd keep me in mind if they turned up any evidence that pointed to me.

The jilted ex would always come under suspicion until they found the real killer. I wasn't naïve enough to think otherwise. All I could do was hope they were found quickly, before they struck again. And if they did kill someone else, it could be dealt with before the press found out. Or the police, for that matter.

What was I thinking? Would I happily hide a murder to save myself the inconvenience? Maybe. It would raise so many questions I didn't have answers for and cast suspicion on the guys as well. If the police started to dig into their pasts, who knows what they would find? Just a wild guess here, but probably things better left buried.

The bus pulled away from the curb and navigated the narrow streets and parked cars before pulling out onto a busier road. Judging by the traffic, we wouldn't be getting to our destination quickly. Whatever.

I was curious to see where we were going, but it was nice to hang out like this for a while.

"Do we get a hint?" Tully sat around and rested his arms on the back of the chair.

"Nope," Zeke said. "Did you bring your passports?"

"We need passports?" Asher frowned.

For a moment, I started to panic. Where was mine? I certainly didn't have it on me.

Zeke grinned. "No. Just figured I would shit stir you all up."

Asher leaned past me to punch Zeke on the arm. "Asshole. Lucky we're not skydiving. I might be tempted to shove you out of the plane without a parachute."

"You would never do that," Zeke said. "You love me too much."

"Depends on how much you piss me off," Asher said, his voice a mock growl. "Penn would help me. Wouldn't you, Penny?"

Penn looked up from his screen. "Huh? Whatever shit you're on about, leave me out of it." He looked back down at his phone.

"Looks like you're on your own there, Ash," Zeke said. "Lucky for me, everyone else in the band loves me."

"Most of the time," Tully said.

"Ouch." Zeke pretended to be hurt, but I doubted the tease caused him any more pain than Asher's punch, which hadn't even made him flinch. "It might be time to think about going solo. Or Abbie and I could form a duo." He gave me a speculative look.

"You'll need a drummer," Asher said. "At least for when you go on tour. I'm in."

"And a lead guitarist," Tully said.

"And bass guitar and saxophone," Channing said.

"You know that defeats the purpose of going solo, right?" Zeke said dryly.

Asher grinned. "It looks like you're stuck with us then."

I noticed Penn hadn't volunteered to join us if we took on this new venture. Fortunately for everyone, it wasn't going to happen. Everyone, that was, but me. Being a part of a band permanently would solve so many problems. On the other hand, it would probably create a few as well.

"That might be the shortest breakup in music history," Zeke said. His expression was reflective but a smile tugged at the corners of his mouth.

"Should we start referring to Abbie as Yoko?" Penn didn't glance up from his screen.

He might have meant that as a joke and he might not, but it stung. The last thing I wanted was to come between the guys. If Wolf Venom broke up someday, I didn't want it to be because of me.

"We're not breaking up," Zeke said. His voice was

tight and his expression at least as pissed off as I felt. Evidently he didn't like the comparison either.

His expression and tone lightened when he spoke again. "If we break up over anything, it will be because of the way the tour bus smells after taco Tuesday. In that case, it will be everyone's fault."

"Except mine," Asher said. "Only pretty smells come out of my ass."

We all broke up laughing, but Penn's accusation lingered in my mind for a long time afterwards.

5

ASHER

"I SHOULD HAVE KNOWN." I thought we were up for a fun day out, or at least a few hours of fun. In retrospect, that was kinda naïve of me. Given the events of the last few days, I really should have guessed what Zeke had in mind. More than that, I should have thought of it first.

Ren pulled the bus up in front of the shooting range and the door groaned open.

Zeke shrugged unapologetically. "We could all use the practice. Whatever is coming for us in the next while, I want us all to be prepared for it." He glanced at Abbie. "Do you know how to shoot a gun?"

She shook her head. "No. I've never even held one."

"We'll teach you," I said. "Zeke is right, we should all be ready. You never know when you might need to shoot Reuben in the cock. Besides, it's fun. Not *jumping up and down on the trampoline in your socks* fun, but still fun."

She didn't look convinced, but she got off the bus and held my hand as we walked into the range. It almost felt like we were boyfriend and girlfriend. Or boyfriends and girlfriend.

As far as I knew, only Zeke and I fucked Abbie, but I knew the rest of them wanted to.

Even Penn, although he wasn't ready to admit it. Even to himself.

Was it weird that none of that bothered me? Often, life goes along the lines of boy meets girl, or boy meets boy, or girl meets girl, or some combination like that. Then they either live happily ever after or they don't.

How often does it go: girl meets six guys and they all live happily ever after? Maybe it was more common than I knew. Now I thought about it, I understood why a lot of people would go for it. There was always someone around when you needed to talk, or fuck, or whatever.

Could a relationship like that happen for us? I couldn't see why not. It wasn't even weird that, in the middle of that, Zeke and I had a thing going on, and Landon and Channing had a thing going on. And all of us still wanted a thing going on with Abbie.

I wondered if Penn and Tully might get it on with each other too. I doubted it. I was almost certain they were straight. Shame, they'd be cute together.

The range was pretty quiet at this time of day. Only a couple of staff were in attendance. They hurried to hand out .22 calibre handguns after most of us pulled out our licenses and flashed them.

The fact none of the staff even glanced at Abbie, much less asked for a license, suggested Zeke called and paid in advance. Probably double or maybe triple the usual fee. That or his brother owned the place, because letting someone in without a firearms license was highly illegal.

Whatever, I'd never tell.

Zeke handed Abbie a Pardini SP pistol and showed her how to use it. The rest of the guys, apart from me, dispersed into their own bays and started to practice.

"We'll try with a twenty-five metre bay." He and I could easily shoot the target at fifty metres, but this was Abbie's first time, so we'd take it easy on her.

"Oh, they have paper targets like in the movies," she said.

I grinned. "It's much more fun if it looks like you're shooting someone."

She raised her eyebrows at me.

"What? I meant it's more fun than shooting at a circle, or a can. Although, shooting cans is fun."

"Only if you're drunk," Zeke said. "Otherwise, it's not much of a challenge."

"You two do this a lot?" She looked slightly alarmed. "Shoot things, I mean."

"Just for practice," I assured her. "We don't go around shooting people."

"If we did, we would be back in our family businesses," Zeke said. "Like Asher said, we do this for practice. The other night, when my brother dropped you off at my place after he abducted you, I could have shot you by accident if I didn't know exactly what I was doing. Handling guns isn't just about hurting people, it's also about making sure you don't hurt people."

"That makes sense," she said. "If I ever picked one up to defend myself, I would probably end up shooting myself in the foot."

"It happens more often than you think," I said dryly.

She cocked a head at me. "Have you shot yourself in the foot?"

I laughed. "No, but I've been tempted to shoot Zeke in the foot every once in a while." I hadn't, but whatever it took to lighten the mood.

"Ironic, I've been tempted to shoot Asher in the cock." Zeke grinned and his eyes dropped lower.

"Because you're jealous of how much bigger I am than you," I teased. "You wouldn't really do that. We'd both regret it if you did." I gave him an intense, heated look.

Using that vibrator on him turned me on so hard I could hardly think at the time. My balls got so heavy they hurt. I badly wanted to use my cock on him, specifically *in* him, but I wouldn't rush. Besides, Abbie's mouth was just as incredible as I knew his ass would be.

Remembering coming down her throat was enough to make my cock twitch.

"I would regret it too," Abbie said. "How about you two make a deal to never shoot each other? Except with water pistols."

I had no intention of shooting Zeke with an actual gun. Likewise, he had no intention of shooting me.

I hoped.

"That should go on the list for summer," I said. "A band water fight. Complete with water balloons. And white T-shirts."

"And no bras," Zeke said.

"Yes, Zeke should definitely not wear a bra," I said jokingly. I swatted his hand away when he went to sock me. "I'm starting to think you're not responsible enough to handle a gun."

"I totally am." Zeke stepped up and took aim at the paper target. "I'll even show you how it's done."

He gave the paper person two new eyes and a hole through their paper heart.

"Is it wrong that I found that hot?" Abbie said.

"I definitely found it hot, and I've seen him do that hundreds of times," I said. "It might be the only thing I will admit that he does better than I do."

"What about singing?" Zeke asked.

I shrugged. "You might be better than me, but I'm not going to admit it." I wasn't a bad singer, but I wasn't anywhere near as good as Zeke and we all knew it. I was okay with that. I was a lot better on the drums than he was. And in the bedroom, if I said so myself.

Give me time, I would teach him all my tricks. And Abbie too.

"Dude, I think you just did." Zeke handed me the

gun. "Let's see if you can do better than me." He gave me a lopsided smile like he didn't think I stood a chance. Dude knew me better than that. I would at least give him a run for his money.

"Challenge accepted." I waited until the paper target was changed out for a new one, and aimed. The poor paper person got three in the chest. I was aiming for a triangle pattern, but didn't quite pull it off. Close enough. If the paper person was real they'd be dead now.

"Not bad," Zeke conceded. "Let's see how well Abbie can do."

Here was where we could get into an argument over who was going to stand behind her and steady her arm. Instead, I leaned against the Perspex between the bays and crossed my arms over my chest.

At some point, if she wanted to learn, I would teach her to play drums. When it came to shooting, Zeke was the better instructor.

Besides, this way I got to stand back and watch.

I won't lie, I would have liked to see him bend her over then and there and slide his cock into her. The thought of the noises she'd make was enough to set my pulse on fire.

Remembering how her mouth and her pussy felt around my cock made my balls throb like I hadn't come in days, not hours. The memory of Zeke's mouth on mine was no less compelling. Between them both, they were going to drive me absolutely wild.

I was at least one million percent here for it.

While Zeke went through the basics of how to aim and fire and deal with the recoil, I pictured the logistics of bending them both over. There were so many interesting combinations we could try. Throw the other guys into the mix and the combinations were endless.

Penn was not only unfair when he suggested Abbie would be the one to break up the band, he was also wrong. If anything, she'd brought us closer together. I doubted I would have been able to act on my feelings for Zeke if it wasn't for her. Even more, I doubted Zeke would have responded the way he did. At least, not as quickly and relatively easy.

Things made more sense with her around.

"Okay, squeeze the trigger gently. Watch out for the recoil. She will bounce back at you faster than a flicked cock," Zeke said.

I held back a chuckle at his analogy. I didn't want

to distract Abbie, especially when she had a weapon in her hand. Surprised people do dangerous things when they're holding a gun.

Abbie squeezed and let out a squeal. "Whoa. I didn't expect it to feel like that."

"That's what I said the first time," I said with a grin.

They both snorted a laugh.

"I was talking about shooting," she said.

My grin widened. "So was I." I couldn't resist putting a hand on my groin.

Both of them followed my hand and swallowed. Yep, the three of us had a vibe going on.

"Try again," Zeke said to Abbie. "It'll be easier now you know what to expect."

She fired again and didn't squeal, which was disappointing because the sound was kinda cute. On the other hand, her knowing how not to shoot me in the head by accident was also cute.

Priorities.

"Good," Zeke said. "Now let's see if you can hit the target." He spoke in soothing, patient tones. More patient than I would be. More patient than any of the guys.

To a greater extent than any of us, he saw what

guns could do in the wrong hands. I'd seen enough. At the end of the day, we both wanted the same thing; for Abbie to be safe.

She aimed again and managed to nick the side of the target's arm.

In the corner of my eye, I watched someone approach. Penn, his hands in his back pockets, a sardonic expression on his face.

I gave him a warning look to discourage him from saying anything nasty. Typically, he ignored it. He was never particularly big on being told what to do, even if it wasn't verbally.

Abbie glanced at Penn over her shoulder.

"Try again," Zeke said. "You need to learn how to shoot even with distractions."

She nodded and aimed again. This time, she nicked the target in the leg.

Penn snorted.

She turned again to give him a dirty look, but he said, "Pretend it's me."

That must have helped, because her next shot got the target right between his legs. If it was a guy, she would have shot his balls off. He would probably bleed out in a few hours.

Poor guy.

"Thinking about my cock," Penn said dryly. "That doesn't surprise me." He turned and walked away.

She didn't deny it.

6

ABBIE

"You did pretty well for your first time," Asher told me over the rim of his coffee cup.

"Thanks." I eyed the open packet of chocolate covered biscuits on the table and debated whether or not I should have another one. "At least I know which way to point it so I don't shoot myself in the face."

He laughed softly. "I'm sure you already knew that. And now you know how to shoot Penn in the dick. Who knows when that skill might come in handy?"

He was so stinking cute and hot at the same time. He was muscular enough that he could be intimidating if he wanted to be. He also had that dangerous edge Zeke had, that undercurrent of violence in everything he did.

"It might be sooner than you think," I said dryly. "Unless he loosens up before the tour starts."

"I don't think Penn knows the meaning of the phrase loosen up," Asher said. "He's wound tighter than one of Tully's guitar strings."

"I've noticed that about him." I gave in and reached for another biscuit. "So, your family is like Zeke's?"

I'd been wanting to ask him about them, but the chance hadn't arisen until now. The press hadn't bothered us for a couple of days, so the guys had gone back to their places or to the gym down the street to work out. I opted to stay in Zeke's townhouse and Asher stayed with me. It was the first time he and I had been alone together.

"Crazy?" Asher asked. "Pretty much. We just have more girls in the family."

"How many siblings do you have?" I bit into the chocolate biscuit.

"There's four of us," Asher said. "Two older than me and one younger. Dane is the oldest. He teaches history at Brutham Academy. He is the wannabe Reuben Brantley of the clan. He's only teaching history until he can regain the family's fortune and favour. Needless to say, I think he'll be teaching for a long time." He shrugged.

"Rose likes to pretend she stays the hell away from all the bullshit. That she's all about the quiet life." He put his empty cup aside and reached for a chocolate covered biscuit.

"But she's involved too?" I asked.

"Up to her eyeballs." He bit into his biscuit and chewed. "She's not open about it. I guess you could say she's the smart one."

"You're smart," I told him.

He grinned. "Thanks, I like to be away from all the bullshit, so I could be the smartest one." He took another bite.

"The DiMarco family was only ever on the edge of things, trying to keep from being caught between the Brantleys and the Bell family. Mostly, we did a crap job of it, but it worked out pretty well for this generation. So far anyway. Except Dane, but that's his problem." He shrugged and bit off a corner of the biscuit.

"And then there's you, and you have another sibling?" I dipped the corner of my biscuit into my coffee and nibbled on it.

Asher sighed and a look of sadnesscrossed his angular face. "Yeah. My younger sister Mina. I guess she wanted to stay away from the bullshit too. She got married at eighteen and shut the rest of us out. She sends us a text message to wish us a merry Christmas every year, but that's all the contact we have with her."

I curled my fingers over his hand. "I'm sorry. Do you miss her?"

"Growing up, she and I were the closest," he said. "In age and, you know, we got on with each other the best. Her nickname when she was a kid was Mina Sunshine, because she was always smiling and laughing. She was sweeter than the rest of us. I guess that's why she shut us out. She's probably living in the suburbs with a bunch of kids by now." He blew out a breath, puffing out his lips.

"Have you tried to contact her?" My heart ached for him.

"Yeah, a bunch of times," he said. "I guess she doesn't want to be found. Zeke has offered to use his family's contacts to look for her. They'd probably find her in an hour, but if she wanted to talk to us she would, you know? She has our numbers and I'm pretty easy to find."

"You miss her but you respect her privacy," I said slowly. "I understand that. I'm not sure I'd be so restrained." Of course, I spent a lot of my time jumping in feet first and then looking, so it stood to reason, if I needed to find a family member by any means, I would do it. And then regret it later.

Asher shrugged. "She's better off living her life away from the family anyway. Her kids will grow up not knowing what their grandparents were involved in."

"They might also grow up not knowing their uncle is a bad ass rock star," I said.

"That is the downside," he agreed. "But their safety is nearly as important as finding out how cool I am." He grinned.

"Nearly," I agreed jokingly.

"What about your family? Are they into anything dubious?" He finished his chocolate covered biscuit and started to lick his fingers clean.

"Probably," I said. "Nothing illegal though." That I knew of. "My parents are retired. I have an older brother, Nathan. He lives in London and works at a bank. And I have a younger sister, Breanna. She's also a singer, but she works as a mechanic during the day."

"Women in greasy overalls," Asher said slowly. "That sounds hot to me."

"Don't tell her that," I said. "She'll either hit you

with a tire jack or make you work for her until you beg her to let you stop."

Bree was an independent woman who hated sexist comments about women in the trades more than anything. I didn't blame her; she dealt with that from the first day of her apprenticeship. It was probably old after the first hour. Still, she stuck it out and proved them all wrong. She was a tougher woman than I would ever be. And an amazing singer.

"I'll be nice," he promised. "I have to think of my hands." He held them up and scrutinised them.

"Wouldn't want those getting dirty," I teased.

"Hell no," he agreed. "Although, it depends on what I get them dirty with." He peered into my cup and found it empty. He took it out of my hands and placed it on the table beside his.

"Does it now?" I watched his every move carefully.

"Yes it does." He took my hand and drew me closer to him.

"Like what?" I asked.

"Like this." He slid his tongue across my lower lip, then back across my top lip. He captured my mouth in a kiss so hot it made my toes curl.

I've always been a big fan of sex, but the more I

was with these guys, the more I wanted them. One kiss and I was already wet and weak-kneed.

"You're so beautiful," he said against my lips.

"No, you," I laughed into his mouth. He was, though. His body was like a statue carved to striking perfection. I would never get tired of looking at him or any of the guys. Every single one of them was a work of art.

"Tasty too." He pulled back and looked at me like he was up to something. Before I could ask, he gently pushed me back on the couch and hooked his fingers in the waistband of my shorts.

I lifted my hips to help him pull them off, and my panties with them.

"See, beautiful." He ran his hands lightly up my legs, to the insides of my thighs. His fingers caressed all around my pussy without sliding in or touching my clit. He looked as though he'd never seen a pussy before and was fascinated by it. Or maybe just that he never got tired of looking at them. Or at mine. I got that, I was never tired of looking at and touching cocks.

"You make me feel beautiful," I said. That was something I could get used to feeling. Not just from him but the other guys too. I felt not only desired, but appreciated. Cared for. Maybe even loved.

"Is that all I make you feel?" He kept on teasing me, almost but not quite touching me where I wanted him to.

"No, that's not all." My hips moved as if they had a mind of their own, seeking his fingers, which continued to evade me.

"What are you feeling now?" He leaned to kiss the inside of my knee.

"Frustration," I said with a throaty laugh. "If you don't touch me soon, I might implode."

"What if I don't touch you?" he asked. "What if this touches you?"

He reached for a chocolate covered biscuit and held it up in front of his face, a sly smile on his lips.

"Asher what are you—"

He put a finger to his lips, then moved it to my knee and slowly spread my legs wider apart. With one hand resting lightly on my belly, he slowly inserted the biscuit into my pussy.

Apart from a slight flash of initial cold, it didn't feel unpleasant. It felt more like he was putting a small vibrator inside me. Without the vibration.

Carefully and with a look of fascinated concentration on his face, he slid the biscuit all the way in, to his fingers. Then back out again. With increasing speed, he started fucking me with the chocolate covered snack. He moved his hand from my belly down to my clit and started tracing circles around and over it. Finally, he fastened two fingers on my clit and started to rub harder and faster.

"You like that?" he asked.

I liked it so much I couldn't respond with words, just with a moan and the bucking of my hips.

"I thought you might," he said. "I want to see you come."

I was already close, but his words pushed me to the edge. I dangled on the precipice for an enticingly long time before I finally tumbled over, muscles clenching around his hand and the biscuit. My back arched and I cried out with pleasure. Stars danced a beautiful ballet show in front of my eyes for a minute, maybe two. I started to come down when another orgasm hit me, this one sweeter and more beautiful than the first.

I cried out again, longer this time, bucking hard against his fingers, needing the sensation to last as long as possible. It could have been a couple of minutes or it could have been an eternity.

Either way, I finally came down and sagged against the fabric of the couch.

His eyes on me, Asher slid the glistening biscuit out of my pussy and took a bite. "It's even tastier like that. I should send a proposition to the people who make them. We could both make a fortune." He grinned.

I shook my head at him while he happily munched on the chocolate covered with my juices. At least life with him would never be boring.

"Would you like some?" He held out the half eaten biscuit.

"No thank you," I replied. If it had his cum on it I might, but not mine. I had a feeling that could be arranged without too much trouble.

"I can think of something else I'd like," I said.

"Yeah?" He raised a speculative eyebrow at me. "What's that?"

"As much fun as a biscuit is, it's not as good as a cock," I said. It was close though, especially when chocolate was involved.

"I was hoping you'd say that." He helped me out of the rest of my clothes and I returned the favour.

When we were both naked, he stretched out over me on the couch and slid his thick cock deep and hard into me.

Yep, definitely better than a biscuit.

7

ASHER

"Shit."

I frowned at my phone. I wanted to ignore the text from my brother, but he would send another one if I did. Or worse, call me.

"What is it?"

I looked from my phone to Abbie's worried face. She really was wildly beautiful. I was certain she didn't realise how gorgeous she was. That was part of her charm. She wasn't conceited or arrogant. She left that to us guys.

"My brother wants to see me. He suggested meeting up for dinner." I tossed my phone onto the coffee table.

"Is this one of those, 'you have no choice' things?" she asked.

"He has a choice," Zeke said from where he sat opposite us, his eyes on his own phone. "He can go to dinner with his brother, or his brother will keep on insisting. Unlike my brother, who would send a car and one of his employees with a gun."

"Dane doesn't like to be ignored," I said. "It's easier to get it over with." After a moment I added, "I'm not sure he wouldn't send a car and a guy with a gun too. I just tend to give in more easily."

I was lucky in that I didn't hate my family the way Zeke hated his. We didn't always get along, but without the kind of power and influence the Brantley family had, there wasn't a lot Dane could do to me.

That didn't mean he wouldn't try if he could get away with it.

"So you're going?" Abbie asked.

"He's going, and so am I." Zeke still didn't look up from his phone. "Neither of us should deal with our families by ourselves. Tell him you'll meet him tonight or tomorrow night. If he wants to hang out with you, it will have to be before the tour starts."

I grabbed my phone and typed a message back to Dane. It didn't take him long to respond.

"Tonight it is," I said. "A couple of hours from now."

Zeke finally lowered his phone. "The three of us should get ready then."

"You want me to come too?" Abbie looked from me to him in surprise, laced with a dose of caution.

I gave her a slow grin. "Love, if I had my way, you'd come all day, every day." I would never get tired of hearing her moan, and watching her hips roll when I touched her.

Likewise with Zeke. I'd be happy to spend the rest of my life curled up in bed with both of them. As long as I could take an hour or two away to perform on stage. That was a whole other rush I wasn't ready to live without.

"We're not leaving you here by yourself," Zeke said. "Dane has no particular reason to see you as a threat. You should be safe enough."

It was the, 'should be' part that worried me, but Zeke was right, we weren't going to leave her here by herself.

Since the night the press camped outside, I'd basically been living here too. My place was just around the corner, so I popped back whenever I needed a change of clothes, but spending time with both of them here felt natural and normal.

"Okay," Abbie said.

She didn't seem even slightly scared about

meeting my brother, even after what I told her about him. While Reuben was inclined to use people or try to make them do what he wanted, Dane was friendly, in the hope it would be to his advantage some day.

That was the problem with my brother. He was like a snake in the grass. You didn't see him until you tripped over him and face planted onto the ground. Or until he bit you.

"Stay on your guard around him," I advised. "You might make the most innocent comment and find later on he uses it against you in some way. He's always looking for an angle or an advantage."

"Why doesn't he work for Reuben?" Abbie asked. "You said he's trying to find ways to get the family back in with the Brantleys, or at least to be more powerful?"

"Reuben doesn't trust him," Zeke said.

"Reuben doesn't trust anyone," I pointed out. "Except for a couple of the men he has working for him." To Abbie I said, "Damon and Gianni are as bad as Reuben."

"If anything, Gianni is worse," Zeke said. "He's not just happy to kill for Reuben, he *likes* doing it. The slower the better. Reuben only kills to get rid of people."

Abbie shuddered. "He sounds charming. What about this—Damon? Does he get a kick out of murder as well?"

Zeke and I exchanged glances.

"Damon is like the best friend you never wanted," Zeke said finally. "He's smooth and slick. Where Reuben thrives on being an asshole, Damon likes to pretend he's nice. Then you let down your guard, just a little bit, and he'll stick a knife between your ribs."

"They both make Reuben sound like a saint," she remarked.

I snorted a laugh. "They do, don't they?"

"They're all as bad as each other," Zeke said. "The evil twins, Hunter and Parker, as well. Those two also thrive on pretending they're nice."

"How do we know you're as nice as you seem?" I asked teasingly.

"Because if I stab either of you with something, it won't be a knife." Zeke grinned.

Those were words guaranteed to make me as hot as hell. Any time he wanted to stab me with his cock, he was welcome to. I knew he knew that. I hoped he would feel comfortable enough to do that sometime soon. Approximately before the anticipation killed me.

"Promises, promises," I muttered.

He gave me a heated look, but changed the subject. "Can you believe the tour starts in three days?"

Abbie suddenly looked nervous. Funny how talking about people killing other people and stabbing was less terrifying than the idea of performing.

Okay, I got it, really. All the shit with our families took place in the shadows. The tour would take place within full view of the entire world. There was absolutely nowhere to hide. Especially for her.

Me—I could sit at the back of the stage and drum, and more or less avoid scrutiny. The press wasn't likely to forget her past or the death of her ex anytime soon. No doubt they would be following her around, waiting for her to do something embarrassing so they could tell everyone how she tripped up. Bloodsucking assholes. I didn't know how they slept at night. Hopefully alone and miserable.

"Part of me wishes it would hurry up, and part of me wishes it was another six months away," Abbie admitted. "I mean, we're ready, after all the rehearsal but..."

"But the press have been assholes to you and you're worried they're going to keep doing it," Zeke said.

"Not just them," she said. "Audiences too. After everything they've heard about me, what if they hate me?" She chewed on her thumbnail with obvious nerves.

"Not a chance," I said with absolute confidence. "They're going to fall head over heels with you the way we have."

"They might turn up with preconceived ideas about me and not even give me a chance," she pointed out. She lowered her hand to her lap and sighed.

I reached over and pulled her to me until she fit neatly under my arm, her head to my chest. "If that's the kind of people they are, we don't want them at our concerts. Believe me when I say our fans are very open and supportive. And you know what, if they don't like you when they walk into the venue, they'll *love* you when they walk out." How could anyone not love her? She was incredible.

"Asher is right, sweetheart," Zeke said.

"Can I get you on video saying that?" I asked teasingly.

He flipped me off. "You're right *this time.*" To Abbie, he said, "Anyway, I'll be here standing beside you, telling the audience how amazing you are. Which won't be necessary, because the moment you sing, they'll forget every single dumbass word the press ever made up about you."

"You make it sound so easy," she said. She nestled in tighter to my chest, like she was trying to absorb my confidence in her. She could have it. I had plenty to spare.

"It is easy, love," I assured her. "You have the full support of the band, the label and even the support act. Violet heard you sing the other day and told me she's jealous you're not singing with Blazing Violet instead of us."

She looked sceptical but Zeke nodded.

"She said exactly that," he said. "I heard all of it. Blaise even agreed with her, and he rarely agrees with anything she says."

"That's true," I agreed. The lead singer and lead guitarist seemed to despise each other, but somehow they worked perfectly well together on stage and in the recording studio. They were like two versions of Penn, difficult as shit but talented as fuck.

"It's too late to arrange that," Zeke said regretfully. "Maybe we could organise something for IslandFest."

Abbie gave him a funny look. "IslandFest?"

"Yeah," I said. "It's a week-long music festival out on an island in the Caribbean. We're booked to play there after the tour is over. We one hundred percent expect you to be there."

"Damn right we do," Zeke said. "What could be better than a week in a tropical resort with a bunch of other bands and all the shenanigans that go down at events like this?" He wiggled his eyebrows.

Yeah, sex on the beach wasn't just a cocktail at events like that. It was just another night.

"If the label still wants me around after the tour is over, I'd love to go." Abbie looked excited.

Hell yeah, I'd like some sex on the beach with her, please and thank you.

"Even if the label doesn't want you around, we do," Zeke said firmly. "But they will. I guarantee it. Levi Jones has never been wrong about an act yet. He has the uncanny ability to pick, well, a winner. Look at Wolf Venom for example. We were a scrappy bunch of guys with a bit of talent and a lot of attitude. We were ambitious but he saw more in us than we saw in ourselves. He put his faith in us and we didn't want to disappoint him. So we didn't."

"You definitely didn't," she agreed. "But I'm pretty sure you would have killed it no matter who you signed with. You guys were always destined for big things."

I squeezed her shoulders. "So were you. You just

met some of the wrong people along the way. But you're with us now, and we are going to help you shine the way you deserve to."

I thought about my words for a moment.

"Is that a new song coming on?" Zeke asked.

"Yes, probably," I said lightly. For both of us, and the rest of the band, who all wrote songs as well, there was always a new song coming on. Inspiration was pretty much everywhere, especially lately.

"You deserve to shine," I sang under my breath. I hummed a few bars.

Zeke and Abbie exchanged amused glances. As if they weren't just as bad as I was at catching a tune at a random moment.

"You laugh now, but it's a guaranteed number one hit," I said.

"You have to write it first, dude," Zeke said.

"A mere formality, dude," I retorted. "After all this time, I would have thought you would've believed in me a bit more." I pretended to pout.

"I do believe in you," he said. "I also know how many unfinished songs you have lying around." To Abbie, he said, "It's lucky he doesn't write novels. If he did, there would be a million different chapter ones and no chapter twos."

"Why are you attacking me like that?" I said, trying to hold back a grin.

Unfortunately, he wasn't wrong. Every time I started to write a song, another three or four popped into my head. Every single one of them demanded to be written right now, so none of them ever got finished. Except the handful that did. One of these days, I would figure out how to focus better. In the meantime, I would comfort myself with the knowledge that the ones I did finish were all really good.

"We should start getting ready to go out for dinner," I said reluctantly. I would have preferred to stay here and let Zeke attack me a bit more. Maybe with his tongue.

8

ASHER

"HE's LATE." I glanced around the restaurant but Dane was nowhere to be seen. Of course not. Leave it to him to make plans and then turn up when he felt like it. Although, he might be lurking in the shadows, waiting to jump out at us, like a tiger hunting its prey.

"Nice place though," Abbie said. She was dressed in a cute little black dress and heels. Her hair was tied back in a simple ponytail and she wore only a touch of make-up.

Her hand brushed mine and I resisted the urge to grab it and never let it go. I didn't, it would be the first thing Dane noticed. We'd already discussed before we got here that we would all play it cool, just in case.

"At least he wasn't early," Zeke said. "If you kept him waiting, he would bitch about it."

"True, true," I said. "I guess that means I get to bitch at him for keeping us waiting." I wouldn't though, because it wasn't worth it. It would only give him the shits and would come back to bite me some day. Dane had a good memory.

I smiled at the server who greeted us with obvious recognition.

She had smiles for Zeke and I, and narrowed eyes for Abbie. Lucky for her, she didn't say anything, just led us to our table and moved away while we got seated.

"I guess she's not a fan," Abbie muttered.

"Don't let it ruin your night," Zeke said.

I grinned. "No, leave that pleasure to Dane."

"You're making him sound like a massive pain in the ass," Abbie said.

"I can neither confirm nor deny that he is a pain in the ass," I said. "You get to make your mind up if he bothers to show."

"He bothered," a voice said behind me. Dane slipped into the chair next to me before I could even turn around.

Anyone seeing us together for the first time could tell we were related. He was slender where I was muscular, but we had the same blue eyes and face shape. He had dark hair like my father and Mina, where I was blond like my mother and Rose. Several people have commented that we both have the same intense stare and resting bitch face.

Dane's gaze swept around the table, taking in all three of us. He gave Zeke a friendly nod, but his eyes lingered longer on Abbie.

I couldn't tell if he recognised her or not, but he clearly admired her. There was no reason why he shouldn't, she was a beautiful woman.

He held out his hand and she shook it.

I did a quick introduction and then jumped right into things.

"Was there something you wanted to talk about?" I didn't see a point in waiting until the end of dinner to get whatever he wanted to get off his chest.

"Can't I want to have dinner with my baby brother?" He gave us all a dazzling smile. If I didn't know him so well, I would have bought it. Who knows, maybe he'd lightened up recently. Stranger things have happened, right?

I gave him a level look. "Maybe, but you look like you have something to say, so you might as well get it over with."

"Were you always so cynical?" Dane asked. He

was still smiling, but a hint of irritation crept into his voice.

"Yes," I said. "I was born cynical. It probably came from overhearing conversations before I was born."

Dane laughed. "I would think you were joking if I wasn't born to the same family. A lot of shit went down back in the day."

"That's an understatement," Zeke said. He looked relaxed and friendly, but none of us were going to forget his father had Dane's and my father killed. There was always going to be a certain level of awkwardness between the two families. Or at least between Dane and Zeke.

Dane had to blame someone and Zeke was often right there in front of his face. He would probably bear the same animosity towards anyone with the last name Brantley.

Ironically, he would also roll over and show his belly if Reuben gave him the chance. He would hold a grudge right up to the moment where it was in his best interest not to.

Dane's eyes flickered over to Abbie.

"She knows everything," I said.

Dane laughed. "Probably not everything. There's a metric shit ton of blood-filled water under the bridge." He stopped talking when a server handed around menus.

I opened mine and skimmed it while I waited for the server to move away.

"She knows enough," I said when it was safe.

"Enough is a dangerous amount," Dane said.

"Better than not enough," Zeke said. "Do you know who Abbie is?"

"In spite of what my brother might think, I don't live under a rock," Dane said. He gave Abbie a warm smile. "Of course I know who Abbie Hart is. I'm a big fan."

"Thank you." She blushed slightly.

Yeah, my brother could be charming when he wanted to be.

"What's your point?" Dane asked. "That I shouldn't know who is going on tour with my little brother?"

I might give him ten points for knowing about that, but he always made it his business to know shit like that.

"We've had a little trouble with some parcels being left on doorsteps," Zeke said.

"Parcels, plural?" Dane asked. "I heard about one of them. Does Abbie have a crazed fan?"

"Is that what this is about?" I asked. "You're

worried about me going on tour with someone who might have a stalker?"

Dane chuckled. "You can take care of yourself, can't you?"

"Thanks for the concern," I said sarcastically. "For your information, yes, we can take care of ourselves. I think what Zeke would like to know is, are you responsible? The other head belonged to Jonah, one of Reuben's henchmen."

"No doubt he deserved it, but I had nothing to do with it," Dane said. He looked indifferent, almost bored, like we were discussing the weather.

I believed him when he said he wasn't involved. Unfortunately. It might have been easier if he was.

The server returned to take our orders, so we fell silent again for a few minutes.

"I assume you want me to keep an ear out for who is responsible?" Dane said once the server moved away. "I'm more than happy to do that. My network has been growing nicely over the last couple of years. You might be surprised the kind of information that comes my way."

I had a feeling this was why we were here.

"Like what?" I asked carefully.

"Like the fact the Bell twins, Chloe and Lila, are

competing with each other to see who will take over the Bell family someday," he said slowly.

I grimaced. "That won't be pretty. How old are they?"

"Eighteen," he replied.

There was something more to his response, but I had a feeling he wouldn't tell me what it was if I asked.

"What has that got to do with us?" Zeke asked.

Dane leaned forward and leaned on his elbows. "I've taken sides."

"Good for you," I said. "I still don't want anything to do with any of this."

"I think we should hear him out," Zeke said softly.

Dane nodded at him. "I've always thought you were the smart one."

"He is," I said. "I'm the hot one."

"We're both hot," Zeke said. He leaned forward towards Dane. "Whose side have you taken and why does it matter to us?"

"I've taken Chloe's," Dane said. "She is the older of the twins. And, I believe, the most capable. Why does it matter?" He cocked his head. "Because your brothers have taken Lila's side."

"I have a lot of brothers," Zeke said. "But I'm going to assume you're referring to Hunter and

Parker, since they go to Brutham and so do the Bell twins."

I blinked a few times.

"I'm sorry," Abbie said. "I don't know what any of this means."

"It means there's going to be a shit storm," Zeke said. "The rivalry between siblings is bad enough, but when you put the Brantley family on one side and the DiMarco family on the other..." He shook his head. "What the fuck were they thinking? I understand you taking sides." He nodded to Dane.

"If you can't get in with the Brantleys, you might as well get in with the Bells," I said.

Dane shrugged unapologetically. "By whatever means necessary."

"My brothers should stay out of any shit involving the Bell family," Zeke said. "We could only end up causing trouble for everyone."

"Because the Brantley family and the Bells hate each other?" Abbie said.

"Exactly," I said. "Let me guess, Reuben is going to be pissed." After a moment I added, "Unless it was his idea?"

Zeke snorted. "Unlikely. I'd bet anything he doesn't know about it."

"He wouldn't ask your brothers to seduce this girl for his own gain?" Abbie asked.

All three of us guys exchanged a glance.

"If she was anyone but a Bell," Zeke said. "Even more than wanting me back in the family, he wants every single one of them dead."

"He's not gonna be impressed with you aligning yourself with Chloe Bell," I told Dane.

He shrugged. "Like you said, if I can't get in with the Brantleys, then I might as well have the Bells at my back."

My brother always did like living dangerously.

"You asked me to come out tonight to warn me?" I said.

Dane shrugged again. "I figured if the shit hit the fan, you'd want to know about it in advance. Especially because of your close association with Zeke."

"That's touching," I said. "You could have stuck to teaching. That would be safer for all of us, especially you." I stared at him for a moment. "Wait a minute, is Chloe your student?" I waved a hand. "Wait another minute, are you sleeping with her? Hold on, don't answer that. She's how much younger than you?" I grimaced.

He chuckled. "Either you want to know or you don't. The fact is, it's none of your business."

"Sounds like a yes to me," Zeke said. "Frankly, I don't give a fuck about your love life. Or your sex life. We appreciate the warning. We'll do our best to stay out of whatever shit the rest of you create."

Zeke massaged his forehead with his fingertips. He looked like he was starting to get a headache. If Dane wasn't there, I would have offered to kiss it better. Right now, that would muddy the waters even more than they already were.

I locked my eyes on Abbie's. She must have thought we were all completely crazy. Maybe we were. Who would be a part of a feuding, mobster family and not run away and hide somewhere far away from them all? Why would Zeke and I chase fame when it brought us into a whole different kind of limelight?

Those were valid questions and I didn't know the answers to them either. I guessed it was that we wanted to live our lives our way and hoped that, at some point, our families would settle down and stop being murderous assholes. That didn't seem like too much to ask, did it?

I didn't think so. I offered her a smile, but it probably looked more like a grimace. I wished we hadn't dragged her into any of this shit to begin with.

"Is this where you say you think I should tell Reuben what Hunter and Parker are up to?" Zeke asked.

"He's going to find out sooner or later," Dane said.

"Either we can tell him," I said slowly, "or we can go on tour and pretend we had no idea. And hope like fuck everything blows over while we're away." I knew which option I preferred.

Zeke sighed heavily. "It seems like we have some talking to do."

9

ABBIE

"WHAT ARE YOU GOING TO DO?" I leaned back on the swing.

We walked home from the restaurant. About half way back, we stopped in a park to enjoy the warm evening.

After the pre-dinner conversation, we only chatted about mundane things and made small talk until the meal was over. Dane didn't seem as bad as Asher made him out to be, but I knew better than to take him at face value. I've met way too many people like him.

"I don't know." Zeke sat on the swing beside me and kicked off the ground.

Asher sat on the other side but seemed content to

rock back and forth gently. "Why do they keep dragging us into their bullshit?"

"I wish I knew the answer to that," Zeke said. "All I have is because they suck."

Asher laughed bitterly. "Yeah, well, I already guessed that much."

"What do you think is going to happen?" I asked. "I mean, they talk about gang wars on the news all the time. People ending up dead and all that. Gun battles in the middle of the street. Innocent people having their houses and cars shot up. Is that where this is leading to?"

"Our families are a little more civilised than that," Zeke said. "It's more likely to lead to poisonings, disappearances or people being shot while they sleep. Those kinds of things. They move around in the shadows, I guess you could say. Like vampires."

"I'm not sure if I call that civilised," I pointed out. "If people end up dead, it's pretty fucking horrible." Depending on the person.

I still couldn't quite bring myself to feel bad about what happened to Vance. If that made me a terrible person, then so be it. At least I wasn't the one wielding... Whatever they used to separate his head from the rest of him.

"It's more civilised because it's less likely to result

in collateral damage," Asher said. "Or having the police identify the family as some sort of organised criminal entity. What they talk about on the news is usually a bunch of street thugs."

I wasn't quite sure I saw a difference, but I didn't bother to say so.

I leaned back and swung a little higher. "I haven't done this in so long." I hadn't stepped foot in a park, much less sat on a swing. It was definitely something I should do more often. It was... liberating. Like I was back in my childhood when I had no cares about anything.

For a little while, I was able to forget about worrying about much of anything.

"I have," Asher said. "But it wasn't this kind of swing."

I caught sight of his grinning face and laughed as I flew past him. "Yeah, well. When you put it that way…"

"I knew I was missing something when I decorated my place," Zeke said. "I'll have to order one when we get back from the tour."

"Hell yeah," Asher said. "Every house should have a sex swing. Or two. And maybe a whole room dedicated to pleasure."

"Isn't that what bedrooms are for?" Zeke asked.

"And kitchens. And bathrooms. And living rooms. And…"

"True," Asher said. "But I meant something more specific. I have a funny feeling you knew that."

Zeke chuckled. "I did know that. You want a dungeon like Tully has."

I almost lost my grip on the chains of the swing. "Dungeon?"

"It's not exactly a dungeon," Zeke said. "Just a room with paddles, feathers, blindfolds and shit like that. It's kinda his thing."

Holy shit, that sounded hot.

I slowed the swing down a little. "Is this a place you go to often?"

"We've been there once or twice," Asher said. "I'm sure he'll be happy to show you around if you ask nicely."

"He'll like it even better if you insist," Zeke said. "Or better yet, let him insist."

"That won't bother you guys?" I asked. Because holy shit, that sounded all kinds of delicious.

"Not at all, sweetheart," Zeke said lightly. "If you're having your needs met, then I'm happy."

"Same here," Asher said. "Paddling and smacking aren't really my thing, but I don't want you to miss out on something you might like."

For the millionth time I wondered who these guys even were and how I got so lucky to meet them. And why, of all women on the face of the planet, they wanted me.

"If I spend time with one of the guys, what will you do?" I asked carefully.

"Are you asking if we'll find other women to fuck?" Zeke asked. "Personally, no. I meant it when I said I was falling for you. Both of you. You two are all I need."

"What he said," Asher agreed. "I'm good with you having a relationship with all of the guys, but I only want to sleep with you two. Not that the other guys aren't hot and all, but the heart wants what the heart wants and all that shit."

"Yeah, it does," Zeke said. "The other guys are like brothers, but that's all they will ever be. Brothers who share my girlfriend."

Girlfriend. I liked the sound of that. It made my heart flutter. That and the idea of having six boyfriends. Was that how this would end up? Hell, it might.

Of course, that included Penn, and I had no real idea where I stood with him. He seemed to like the possibility I was thinking of his cock at the shooting range. There might be some hope for us some day.

"Brothers and boyfriend who share your girl-friend," Asher said. He sounded tentative, like he wasn't quite sure that was a step too far for Zeke.

"Yes, that," Zeke said. "My girlfriend Abbie, my boyfriend Asher, and me. That sounds pretty fucking awesome to me." He nodded firmly as I swung past.

"To me too," I agreed. I leaned back and looked towards the sky, letting the swing move back and forth slowly. Even though I couldn't see the stars past the city lights, it was still the perfect night. A nice dinner, two incredible guys and a relaxing swing in the park. What else could a girl want?

"How many times has that car gone past?" Asher asked.

Of course it couldn't last.

"At least three," Zeke said. "Don't stop swinging," he added quickly as I went to put my feet on the ground to stop myself. "It could be nothing, but if it isn't we need to play it cool."

"What do you think it is?" I tried not to panic. It could be anything from a lost driver, to someone ready to shoot us as they drove past, or even the press lurking around us. I couldn't rule out that it might be the killer searching for another head.

"I don't know," he said. "We'll give it a few

minutes, then leave as though that was exactly what we were planning all along. Let the swing slow down by itself."

"Okay." I stuck my legs out in front of me and let the momentum gradually die away.

My heart was racing and my palms were so slick it was hard to cling onto the chain. Flying off and landing on my ass on the rubber under the swing would definitely not be the definition of playing it cool.

"All right, they've gone around a corner," Zeke said. "As casually as you can, get off the swings. Talk, laugh, just act naturally."

I lowered my feet and ran a few steps before I was able to bring the swing to a full stop.

"That was fun," I said more loudly than I probably should have. "We should do that another time."

"We should." Zeke drew me to him and tucked me under his arm.

"I'm trying to think of a joke, but nothing is coming to mind," Asher said. He walked close to the other side of me, so our hands brushed against each other every so often.

"We could talk about how our cocks are so much bigger than everyone else's," Zeke said.

Asher grinned. "That's not a joke, it's true."

"We all know that, but talking about it will make us look like we're not suspicious about strange, dark cars gliding past in the middle of the night," Zeke said.

"True," Asher agreed. "We could talk about getting some chocolate sauce and dribbling it all over Abbie. And then licking it all off."

"I like that conversation," I said. "We could also dribble it on one of you and the other two could lick it off." The downside to being covered in chocolate sauce myself was that I wouldn't get to taste it.

"We could have a bath in chocolate," Asher said. "Or champagne."

"I don't know, wouldn't that be sticky?" I said.

He shrugged. "I don't know. It would be fun to find out."

"Any sign of it?" I asked. A white van and a light-coloured hatchback passed by, but neither slowed.

Asher grabbed my hand to stop me from walking, turned and kissed me. When he pulled back, he glanced over my shoulder.

"Don't look back, but it's parked by the side of the road. I can't get a good enough look to see if anyone's in it. If they are, the doors are closed. If they're coming for us, they're not doing it yet."

We went on walking.

"It could be Reuben has sent someone to intimidate us," Zeke said.

"I hate to say it, but it's working." I was trying hard not to freak the fuck out. "It would look really bad if we started running, wouldn't it?"

"Absolutely," Zeke agreed. "Not only would they know we know they're there, they would also know they have us worried."

"Only worried?" I asked. "I think I'm going to pee my panties." Ruining them was one thing, this was something else completely different and definitely not welcome.

"Yeah, that's really not how we want you wet," Asher said.

"If they wanted us dead, we'd be dead," Zeke said. "And if they were planning to abduct us, they would have done that too. They might be people going about their lives."

"Do you believe that?" I asked. I hoped he'd say yes, but I knew he wasn't going to.

"Not really." He shrugged. "But I'm not gonna let myself be intimidated either. If that's what Reuben thinks, he can go to hell."

It was difficult to resist the urge to look back, but I managed to control myself. If Zeke was right and this was an attempt to scare us, then I had to try not to look scared. Easier said than done. I couldn't forget the way the evil twins bundled me into the back of a car so Reuben could have a conversation with me.

"Is this his last chance to try to get to you before the tour?" I asked.

Zeke snorted softly, which wasn't the response I was hoping for. "He won't let up just because we're out of Sydney. He likes to remind me he has a long reach."

"I'm starting to wish I'd kicked him in the dick when I had the chance." I huffed.

Both guys chuckled.

"Please don't do that unless I'm there to see it," Asher said.

"Me too," Zeke agreed. "And if you do that, you better be ready to run like hell. Otherwise he'll come after you or send one of his men. You don't want to get on the wrong side of Damon or Gianni."

"I'll bear that in mind," I said. They certainly didn't sound like people I wanted to meet, much less cross. Hunter and Parker were bad enough.

I startled at the sound of a car engine approaching slowly.

"Don't look back," Zeke urged.

I had been just about to do just that.

My heart raced harder. I had the sinking feeling I was about to die here on a Sydney street in the middle of the night. That was not how I wanted to die.

The car drew even with us and stayed there for a good ten or twenty heartbeats.

A moment before I gave in to panic, it slipped past us and roared away into the night.

10

ABBIE

"THIS NEVER GETS OLD." I stood at the edge of the stage in the biggest stadium in Sydney and looked out at the floor and chairs which were currently empty. The place looked like it would fit at least a billion people.

In reality, it fit about eighty thousand, which was pretty close to a billion, as far as I was concerned.

"It really doesn't," Tully agreed. He stood a couple of metres away, his guitar on a strap around his neck. "Everything else we do leads up to concert nights. At least, that's how I see it. Making albums, all the interviews and shit, it's all so we can get to this."

"I agree," I said. "Nothing compares to perform- ing. Although, sex comes pretty close."

I couldn't help thinking about what the guys told me about Tully and his room. There was no time to ask about it now, or insist. This morning's sound check was the official start of the tour. I was excited as fuck, and not at all sad to leave Sydney behind for a while.

He gave me a lopsided smile. "If you think performing is better than sex, then you might be having sex with the wrong people."

"I heard that," Asher called out from the back of the stage.

"Me too," Zeke said from the side.

Penn looked over his shoulder at them from where he stood in front of his keyboard. He grimaced, then looked away. Surprisingly, for once, he had no smart ass comment to make. Or maybe he'd kindly save it until later.

Tully grinned. "Did I hit a nerve? Sorry, not sorry."

Something clattered to the ground at his feet. It took me a moment to realise Asher had thrown one of his drumsticks at him.

Tully crouched and snatched it up before throwing it back.

Asher managed to catch it before it hit him in the face. "Hell yeah, I have mad catching skills."

"Makes up for the fact you can't throw for shit," Landon teased.

Asher waved the drumstick at the bassist. "Don't make me get up, come over there and whip your ass with this."

"As if you could, old man," Landon scoffed playfully.

"Who are you calling old man?" Asher asked. "You're only a couple of years younger than me."

"And yet I'm so much wiser than you are." Landon swung his bass guitar strap over his head and settled the bright purple instrument into place.

"In your dreams," Asher retorted.

"You guys are all full of shit," Penn said.

"See, Penn is the wise one," Channing said. "He is well aware how full of shit you all are."

"Who says I wasn't including you in that?" Penn asked.

"I do," Channing said. "Wait, you think I'm full of shit too? I'm hurt." He put his saxophone to his lips and played a sad tune.

"You'll get over it," Penn said.

"Says you," Channing said. "I think I might be scarred for life."

Penn rolled his eyes at him and turned back to his keyboard.

I caught Zeke's grin and smiled back before I stepped away from the edge of the stage. He pulled his microphone out of the stand and turned it on.

"Anyone not in the band should get off the stage for soundcheck." Penn had looked back up from his keyboard and was now looking right at me. He had so much disdain on his face, I almost backed up a step.

"I'll wait in the wings," I murmured. I felt a bit like a kicked dog. Lucky for him I didn't turn around and bite him.

He looked like anywhere in the stadium would be too close, but he turned away. Evidently he knew getting me off the stage was as good as he was going to get.

All of the guys looked like they wanted to tell me to stay, but in the end, Penn was right. I wasn't a member of Wolf Venom. This was their soundcheck, not mine. I would get my time on stage before them and with them, but not now.

Zeke gave my hand a quick squeeze as I walked past him. "Let us know if we suck."

"You could never suck. Not your music anyway." I managed a small smile, slipped my hand out of his and hurried down the steps to the space behind the stage.

From there, I could walk around to where the audience would stand, or slip into a seat. It wasn't every day a girl got a private concert from one of the biggest bands in the world, even though it was only a soundcheck. Honestly, I would take what I could get.

They started up playing and I moved to get out of the way of a couple of the tour staff.

They gave me a smile and nod, and hurried on with what they were doing. At least they were friendly. And professional.

"They're pretty awesome, aren't they?" Violet Fletcher-Jones and Blaise Turner appeared from down the corridor.

She wore skin tight black jeans and an equally tight black T-shirt. Her hair was coloured to match her name, and she wore boots with heels so high she was almost as tall as Blaise. Without the extra height, she would be lucky to come up much past his shoulder. What she lacked in height she made up for in personality.

"Yeah, they're pretty good," I agreed. More than pretty good, but I didn't want to overdo it.

Blaise snorted. "Pretty good? Jesus Christ." He gave me a look that reminded me of Penn, but with a lot less dislike. He seemed to save that expression for Violet.

"I don't want to sound like a fangirl," I said. Or a groupie. I was officially dating two of them, so I should be well beyond either of those things.

"You don't," Violet said. "Just ignore him. He got out of bed on the wrong side about twenty years ago and never changed."

Blaise rolled his eyes. He looked like he would have told her to fuck off if I wasn't there. He had more restraint than Penn at least.

"You must be excited about tonight," she continued. She looked as though she was barely able to stand still.

"I really am," I agreed. "I'm sure you guys are too." I glanced around but couldn't see the other band members. No doubt they wouldn't be too far away.

"I'd be more excited if we were headlining like we should be." Blaise gave Violet a glance like it was her fault somehow.

If there was more to that story, I was probably better off not knowing. It might be something private between them. Or between them and the rest of the band.

"We will be," she told him, her tone terse. "This tour is the biggest thing we've ever done. It's going to be an amazing learning experience for all of us."

He grunted. "We know enough."

She shrugged. To me she said, "If you ever want to go out and get a drink, just us girls, let me know. Sometimes it's nice to get away from all the testosterone, if you know what I mean." She gave Blaise a sarcastic smile.

He responded with a matching one that Penn would have been proud of.

"Yes, I do," I agreed. While I adored the guys, it was nice to talk to another woman once in a while. Candy and I had started to text each other regularly, and made plans to hang out when the tour was over, but it would be nice to have a female friend during the tour.

Although, my blond hair was boring in comparison to their bright pink and bright purple. Maybe I should colour mine blue or something.

"That would be great," I said sincerely. "Hopefully we can fit in some sightseeing here and there too." I knew there wouldn't be much time for that, except out the window of a bus, car or van. Or a plane. But what time I could find, I would try to take it.

Violet grinned. "I want to make sure we see the Eiffel Tower and some American football. Maybe some soccer when we're in England."

"It's also called football," Blaise said. "If you call it soccer in England, they will crucify you."

She shrugged. "Whatever. Kicking a ball around on the grass." She waved a hand in dismissal.

I got the distinct impression she was trying to bait him. Judging by the expression on his face, it was working. Even in the dim light down here, his face looked a little pink.

"All of those things sound like fun," I said. "Maybe we can see a hockey game while we're in Canada. I have a couple of friends who live on the eastern side. I know one will be happy to take us. She pretty much lives to go to hockey games."

"I like that idea," Violet said. "What could be better than hitting a ball with a stick?" Her perfectly shaped eyebrows wiggled up and down a couple of times.

Blaise grunted with disgust. "In case you hadn't guessed, Violet knows nothing about sports. She likes to go and watch it to see the men running around and getting sweaty."

We both looked at him like we couldn't work out what the problem was.

He looked from one of us to the other and back again, then shook his head. "You fucking women are all the same."

"Awesome?" Violet asked. She smiled sweetly.

"That sounds accurate to me," I said. "For the

record though, I like to go to sporting events for the atmosphere. The sweaty men part is a bonus." Admittedly, it was a pretty good bonus.

Speaking of sweaty men, I glanced back up the stairs for a glimpse of the guys. Zeke moved around the front of the stage, singing as though he had a whole audience to perform to.

When I thought about it, he probably did. People already started lining up outside in the middle of the night, in the hope of getting a front row spot. No doubt they were listening from the outside and getting excited. Singing along, dancing and enjoying the whole pre-concert experience.

I'd done exactly that more times than I could count. Being on the inside was more exciting, but being out there was a shit load of fun.

"I can't wait to get out there," Violet said. "I'm so full of adrenaline right now, I could run around the whole arena and it would barely take the edge off."

"Why don't you then?" Blaise asked. "I'll take over as lead singer. I'm sure no one would notice."

She rolled her eyes at him. "They would notice when they heard a voice that sounded like a cat having its tail pulled."

"Fuck off," he retorted. "I sound better than that."

"Yeah, a little bit," she agreed.

I wondered how long it would be before they slept together. It was pretty obvious, at least to me, they had it bad for each other. Did Penn and I come across that way? I'm sure myself and all the other guys did at least. If these two got it together, they might set the world ablaze. Pun totally intended.

I turned my attention to listen to the guys, with my professional ear. The sound in the stadium was amazing, of course. They were built to have perfect acoustics as well as the space to get lots of bums on seats and feet on the ground.

A shiver of excitement passed through me. Tonight, I'd either start to put my career back on track, or I would spectacularly fall flat on my face.

I hoped to hell it was the first.

11

ASHER

"Thank you, Sydney! We're Blazing Violet. You guys were fucking fantastic!"

Violet gave a last wave to the crowd, put the microphone back in the stand and headed off the stage with the rest of her band.

She gave us all high-fives as she passed us by. Everyone except for Abbie, who she hugged.

When did that happen? I didn't realise they were friends. That was awesome. Maybe I was biased, but I wanted everyone to like Abbie as much as I did. She deserved it. And it made everyone's lives easier if we all got along.

Speaking of getting along... I looked over to Penn.

His face was turned towards the stage. For once,

he wasn't scowling. He wasn't smiling either. He looked lost in his thoughts.

In spite of what people thought, there was a decent guy deep down. Not even that deep, to be honest. He'd been through a lot, and put up stone walls around himself. Once in a while, he'd open up and show the real him. That hadn't happened recently. He was shut down tighter before a tour. Hell, we all were. None of us wanted to fall on our faces. Even now, the fear of failure hung heavy over us. Impostor syndrome happened even to the best of us.

He must have sensed I was watching; he turned and looked at me. The sides of his mouth drew back slightly before he turned and looked away.

The last few weeks were hectic to say the least. I got caught up in releasing the album, preparing for the tour and getting to know Abbie. I hadn't had the time to make sure the rest of the guys were okay.

We were usually good at looking out for each other. I made a mental note to try to do better.

"You're up," Zeke said to Abbie. "Don't worry, you're going to be amazing."

"Break a leg," Penn said with an ironic smile.

She looked like she wanted to flip him off.

Instead she smiled sweetly. "You too, when it's *your* turn on stage."

He narrowed his eyes at her like he was angry, but there was an underlying current there. Like all he really wanted to do was drag her off to bed.

Honestly, she had the same expression on her face.

"Phew, it's hot in here." Landon fanned his face with his hand. Evidently he was catching the same vibe. It was hard not to catch it, it was electric.

"You'll be incredible," I told Abbie, if only to change the subject. "They're going to love you."

She flashed me a nervous smile and then hurried up the steps towards the stage.

The keyboardist and guitarist the label booked to play with her were already in place, waiting for her. I would have liked to play with her, but we'd get our chance.

Besides, having all women on the stage was cool. Jewel Ruby and Macquarie Tanaka were some of the best the label had. Of course. They didn't have anyone who wasn't incredible.

Okay, I might be biased about that too.

Abbie grabbed the microphone out of the stand and checked it was on. She looked anxious but excited.

I hoped to hell the audience would accept her. Eighty thousand asses was a lot to kick if we needed to.

"Good evening, Sydney," she said into the microphone. "I'm new in town. I'm sure you've never heard of me, but I hope we can be friends."

The applause and cheers that met her words weren't as enthusiastic as those that followed Blazing Violet off the stage, but I didn't hear any boos or jeers.

It was a start, right?

She gave Jewel and Macquarie a smile and a nod and they started to play. After a moment, she lifted the mic to her lips and started to sing. It took her a bar or two, but she quickly found her groove and started to have fun.

By the end of the song, the audience was joining in, singing and clapping. It wasn't quite with the same warmth and fervour they showed when we performed, but it could have gone a lot worse.

She finished her last song and gave the audience a wave.

"Thank you, Sydney. Are you looking forward to seeing Wolf Venom?" She turned her ear towards the audience. "What? I can't hear you. *Are you looking forward to seeing Wolf Venom?*"

The crowd went wild cheering, clapping and stomping their feet.

I grinned. It was impossible not to get caught up in the excitement, in spite of the flutter of nerves. That always happened before the start of the tour; the combination of anticipation and terror.

By the end, I'd be too tired to be nervous.

"Should we bring them out?" Abbie asked.

Again, the audience cheered and roared.

She grinned. "They might need a bit more encouragement. They're all super shy."

She laughed into the microphone and the audience laughed with her. Everyone in the room knew we were far from shy.

"Tell them to come on out," she told the crowd.

Eighty thousand people shouted simultaneously, *"Come on out!"*

"I guess we better go out there." Zeke shook his head and laughed. He started up the steps and the rest of us followed.

The audience went absolutely crazy.

Zeke pulled out the microphone from the other stand and slipped an arm around Abbie's waist. "Abbie Hart, ladies and gentlemen. Isn't she something fucking else?"

His words were met with a bigger cheer than most of hers, but she smiled in response.

"Wolf Venom is something fucking else," Abbie said into her own mic. "Blazing Violet and I were just keeping them warm for you."

"That's nice of you." Zeke walked over to the side of the stage, grabbed a bottle of water and took a gulp. "What do you say we give them a little something special?"

The glance she gave him sent my mind plunging straight my cock.

"Oh yeah?" she said. "You have something in mind?"

"Yeah, do you know the words to 'Take Me Down Lower'?" He put the bottle down and stepped back to the middle of the stage.

"I think I've heard of it," she said as if they hadn't practiced the song a hundred times before.

"I'll start, see if you can catch up." He grinned.

That was our cue to start playing.

Zeke sang to the first chorus before Abbie joined in.

The audience was a lot more receptive to her by now and cheered when she sang.

She was a lot more relaxed as well. When the song ended and she put her microphone back on the stand, she looked disappointed. She would come back near the end for her second song, but until then, she would be watching from backstage.

She flashed me a smile before she disappeared down the steps.

My eyes weren't the only ones which followed her off the stage. All of the guys did except for Penn, whose back was to her.

She was replaced by Isaac, one of the guys from the label.

Phone in his hand, Isaac started to move around the stage, recording us to share on social media. Fans got a kick out of watching sneak peeks of our concerts from different places all over the world. It was the closest thing to being there we could offer them. Plus, some of us secretly got a kick out of watching the footage back. Like me.

I grinned at the phone as Isaac pointed it at me, and added a bit more grooving to my playing. I didn't want the audience to think I only played the drums, I wanted them to think I looked cool doing it.

People often commented that I made it look easy. After so many years of playing, it was second nature. Especially with the songs we'd played for years. I could have played them in my sleep.

Isaac moved past me and focused on Landon, who of course *had* to arch his back and raise his bass guitar to show off his skills. He pursed his lips as he played, adding another layer of cool to his performance.

There was, after all, more to being a part of a rock band than just the ability to make music. You had to be willing and able to perform, even when under pressure. Some may say *particularly* when under pressure. Eighty thousand people were watching us right now. If the idea freaked any of us out too much, we were in the wrong profession.

I looked out at the audience. Most looked around my age, but a few were younger and a few were older. Most wore T-shirts with the Wolf Venom logo on it—a wolf's head with glowing green eyes and protruding tongue. White liquid trickled and dripped off the end of the tongue.

Because we're mature, we joked that it could be cum, beer or whiskey, but it was supposed to be venom. Either way, it looked pretty fucking awesome to me.

One of the guys in the audience was wearing a banana costume, which was pretty fucking awesome too. When Isaac reached him, he held the phone toward him for a couple of seconds. Banana-guy was going to get a big kick out of watching that back later on.

Hell, I was gonna get a kick out of watching it back later on. It wasn't every day you saw a guy in a banana costume. It must be hot as fuck under there.

Isaac followed Zeke around the stage for a while, before he stepped down the side of the stage to film the audience.

"Are you having fun, Sydney?" Zeke shouted into his mic.

They roared in response.

"Great. We have a little surprise for you. Don't go anywhere." He slipped his microphone into the stand. We all put down our instruments and headed towards the steps.

Everyone except for Penn.

"What's going on?" Abbie asked when we stepped down toward her. She looked worried. Evidently this was a surprise for her too.

Zeke grinned and removed off his sweat drenched T-shirt. "Just a little something we added since the last tour."

She looked confused but mostly distracted by the sight of Zeke's sweaty torso before he pulled on the dry tee a staff member handed him.

Understandable, the view was pretty fucking awesome.

I managed to tear my eyes off him and changed my shirt before I slipped an arm around her and tucked her close to my side.

"You'll love it," I told her. I hoped the crowd did. This was a risk, like adding Abbie to the lineup. It could be the best choice ever, or a major fuck up. I knew which one I was voting for.

Penn sat in front of his keyboard and waited until the audience was silent. Okay, as silent as eighty thousand people could be.

Isaac climbed back onto the stage to film him.

My heart raced with anticipation. For Penn's sake, I hoped this went down well. If it didn't, he'd be angrier than a drop bear all tour. Only real, because drop bears are an urban myth to scare tourists.

Penn placed his hands on the keys and leaned towards the microphone.

With the attention of everyone in the stadium, he started to sing Hallelujah, just him and his keyboard.

"I didn't know he could sing," Abbie whispered.

"If it's music related, he can do it," I whispered back. And he did it well.

The audience was quiet through the whole thing, enraptured by the moment he created.

There was no doubt in the mind of anyone there that he was born to perform. He captured everyone's attention from the first note to the very last.

If I was ever jealous of anyone, it was him and his innate musical ability. The band was fucking lucky to have him, and he knew it.

When he was finished, the crowd burst into their wildest applause yet.

"Wow," Abbie breathed. "That was…"

"Hot?" I suggested. I turned and locked eyes on her.

"I was going to say awesome, but hot works too," she agreed.

I smiled and gave her a quick kiss before I hurried back onto the stage.

After all, we couldn't let Penn have all the limelight, right?

ABBIE

"THAT WAS FUCKING FANTASTIC." Violet toasted all of us with a shot of vodka, then tossed it back.

After the concert, we were all ushered into limousines and driven to Zodiac Underground, the club owned by a guy named Will Holding.

According to Zeke, Will was Levi's best friend. He assured me we would be well taken care of and the label would pick up the bill later.

They had me at free alcohol.

"Most valuable player of the concert has to go to Mr Beauregard Pennington," Landon declared. "We would all take our hats off to you if we were wearing hats." He threw back a shot of tequila.

Penn shrugged and almost looked pleased at the

praise. Almost. "Just doing my job," he said with a grunt.

"You kicked ass," Channing said. He was sipping on a beer with more restraint than his boyfriend.

"You really did, my friend." Zeke tapped him on the shoulder. "I better be careful or the label will give my job to you. Or worse, you'll leave the band and go solo."

"Fuck that," Penn muttered. "Too much pressure. If I wanted that I would have stuck with the Conservatory of Music."

"Nah," Asher said. "Your talent would have been wasted there."

I would have agreed, but I suspected if I said anything, it would bring down Penn's mood. This was his moment, I didn't want to take it away from him.

In the end, the choice was taken out of my hands when Asher said, "Let's give a special mention to Abbie, who also kicked ass." He held up his whiskey and cola to toast me. "That should shut the press up now."

He looked so adorably proud my heart skipped a beat or two.

"Both of their performances should," Zeke said quietly, but equally proud.

I knew what he was referring to, we all did. In the past, the press had been as shitty to Penn as they were to me. Although, I was an innocent bystander in the shit that happened to me. The things he did…

I pushed it out of my mind. It didn't matter now. The past was the past. No one wanted to live there. I certainly didn't.

"When did you guys plan Penn's solo?" I asked Zeke, who sat beside me at the large table. Technically, it was several tables pushed together, but whatever. "No one mentioned it at rehearsal." I wondered if I should be mad at them for keeping that a secret, but decided against it. It was a wonderful surprise, and at the end of the day, the band's secret to keep. I didn't need to know everything they did, all the time.

He shrugged. "It's something we've had in the works for a while now. It's a good chance for me to get a toilet break." He grinned.

Penn flipped him off. "Yeah, that's the only reason I'm doing it," he said sarcastically. "So you can think of me while you're holding your dick."

"Do you *want* us to be thinking about you?" A smile tugged at the corners of Asher's lips.

"I'm fucking unforgettable," Penn said. "I wouldn't blame you if you did."

I tried not to snort too loudly. He wasn't wrong. He was one of the more memorable people I knew.

He turned, narrowed eyes on me. "Who got the bigger applause? Me or her?"

I opened my mouth to retort, but Zeke put his hand on my arm.

"Let's not fight, okay? It's going to be a really long tour if we start on the first night."

I sat back and closed my mouth.

Penn smirked and turned away.

Asshole.

Zeke took his hand off my arm and rested it lightly on the back of my neck instead. He looked thoughtful.

"Should I be worried?" I asked.

His brow creased. "Worried about what, sweetheart?"

"The expression on your face. You look like you're up to something." I picked up my glass of wine and took a sip. I wasn't in the mood to get plastered tonight. A light buzz was enough, especially after a big concert. That was all the lift I needed.

"Do I?" He gave me a smile like he was definitely planning something. "Don't worry, it won't be anything bad." He paused for a beat, then added, "I don't think it's bad. Other people might disagree." His brows twitched.

"What are you plotting?" Asher asked from the other side of me.

"World domination," Zeke said lightly. "What else?"

"That's not your world domination face," Asher said. "That's your, 'I'm going to run something by the label and it's going to be epic,' face."

He chuckled. "I have different faces for those two things?"

"Yes," Asher said. "They're two of my favourite faces." He grinned. "You can guess what my first favourite face is."

"The one I have when I'm about to hand you a fresh cup of coffee?" Zeke asked.

"That's definitely in my top four," Asher said.

"Orgasms!" Violet suddenly shouted. "That's your favourite face, isn't it?"

Everyone turned to her and laughed. She was going to have one hell of a hangover in the morning, but she was clearly enjoying herself.

"She's right," Asher said. "That's my favourite expression on anyone's face, especially mine."

"That gives a whole new meaning to the expression 'cum face'," Tully said.

"Cum face is an expression?" Landon asked. "Is that like cockhead?" He blinked like his intoxicated brain was trying to make sense of what Tully said, but couldn't quite manage.

"No," Tully said. "It's more like, 'oops, I missed coming in your mouth and got it all over your face instead.'"

"Oh." Landon nodded. "That makes sense." He still looked confused.

I watched Tully while he spoke and thought again about the room the guys mentioned. Only now, my imagination extended to Tully squirting cum over my cheeks and chin. The idea made me feel all warm inside.

"How do you miss coming in someone's mouth?" Asher asked. "You must have really shit aim." He was also showing signs of how much he'd had to drink.

Tully picked up a slice of cheese from a bowl in the middle of the table and threw it at Asher. It landed squarely in the drummer's drink with a plop.

"What the fuck, Tull?" Asher pulled out the cheese and flicked it back at Tully. It flew past the lead guitarist and landed somewhere on the floor.

"Who has shit aim?" Tully laughed.

"Still you, cockhead," Asher retorted playfully.

Zeke shook his head at them. "Some day they'll grow up, but today is not that day."

"I've heard a rumour," Asher said, suddenly serious. "Apparently, growing up is overrated. I plan on never finding out." He nodded so firmly he might have fallen off his chair if there wasn't a table in front of him.

Zeke shot an arm out to steady him and pressed him against the back of his seat.

"Thanks, babe," Asher muttered.

"Ash, dude, that is the smartest thing I've ever heard you say," Landon said. "I'm not gonna grow up either."

"Me three," Channing agreed.

"Yeah, leave all the adult shit to Penn, Tully and I," Zeke said. "And Abbie." He gave me a speculative look.

"Fuck nope," I said. "So far, growing up is overrated as fuck. Hard pass."

I wouldn't go back to my childhood either. Could I choose a point where I was more innocent than right now, but old enough to do things for myself? That sounded like bliss to me.

"I don't want to be an adult either," Tully declared. "I'm happy to defer to you and Penn. As long as you don't try to impose an early bedtime, or stop me eating cake for dinner."

"When have you ever eaten cake for dinner?" Zeke laughed.

"Never," Tully said with a nod. "But I want to be able to, if I feel like it."

"Noted," Zeke said. "Tully can hereby eat cake for dinner whenever he wants."

"Can I eat it off Abbie?" Tully asked.

That question took me by surprise and actually made me blush.

"What flavour?" Yeah, that was the important thing here wasn't it? I resisted the urge to slap my hand across my eyes.

Tully cocked his head at me. "I'm pretty sure you would taste good with any flavour, but maybe something with lemon in it."

Penn grunted something that sounded like disapproval, but he was ignored by everyone else at the table. Presumably he didn't like lemon flavour. Yeah, that was it.

"That sounds accurate," Zeke said. "Wouldn't you say, Asher?"

"Lemon or chocolate," Asher agreed. "But she tastes pretty good without any flavouring as well."

A month ago, I would have been embarrassed to

have people talk about me like that. No, maybe embarrassed wasn't the right word. I would have felt uncomfortable, and thought they were just trying to be nice.

Now, I felt a lot more confident and knew they were describing me the way they saw me. Or tasted me. I actually liked hearing it now.

A girl could get a healthy ego at this rate.

"Talented and delicious," Zeke said. "That's one hell of a combination."

"That description fits you too," Asher told him. He gave Zeke the most adoring look.

They were just so fucking cute together. The three of us together made one hell of a combination.

"And you," I said before anyone thought this conversation was making me uneasy. "Both of you."

"I think I'm going to be sick," Violet declared. She clapped a hand over her mouth, stood and ran from the table towards the toilets.

"What she said," Penn said with a grunt. "I have *not* had enough alcohol for this conversation."

"And Violet had too much," Blaise said, speaking up for the first time in an hour or two. "Whereas I've had just enough." He toasted me with what I thought was bourbon, and a grin.

I knew he wasn't interested in me in that way, but

all the talk about taste and cake was pretty interesting.

I grinned back at him. "I have a feeling this tour isn't going to be boring." Absolutely bat shit crazy maybe, but not boring.

Luckily, I liked a bit of bat shit crazy in my life.

"That is for fucking sure," Asher said. "It's going to be one hell of a ride and I'm here for every second of it." He put his hand up to Tully and they high-fived each other.

"Me too, babe." Zeke grinned.

I wondered if he'd decided to talk to Reuben about the evil twins and their relationship with Lila Bell.

Every now and again I caught him with a frown on his face. He was obviously thinking about it, and troubled. It didn't seem fair to have a heavy burden on his mind when he should be thinking about, and enjoying, the tour. I wished there was something I could do to help, but short of trying to find Reuben Brantley's phone number and contacting him myself, all I could do was be here for Zeke when he needed me.

"Are you okay?" I asked him softly.

"Yeah," he replied.

He shook his head and his dark expression lifted.

"If I haven't mentioned it recently, you were mind blowing tonight. Fans are going to be talking about that concert for the next fifty years at least. Grandchildren will be impressed their grandparents were there."

I snorted a laugh. "You make it sound like the moon landing."

He grinned. "It's way bigger than the moon landing. And it actually happened."

"I didn't take you for a conspiracy theorist." I finished the last of my wine.

He shrugged one shoulder. "I'm not, I just know we were out of this world."

I groaned at his pun. "Is that why you're the adult here? Because of the dad jokes?"

He rubbed the back of his head. "I'm practising."

"For being a dad?" The idea made my heart jump a little bit. I hadn't thought where children might fit into this arrangement, or even if they could. It would certainly complicate things a lot more.

He grinned slowly. "Or a daddy."

That was a whole other conversation.

13

ABBIE

"THERE'S SOMETHING ABOUT MELBOURNE." I sipped my coffee and enjoyed the view of the Yarra River out the window.

"It's one of my favourite places to hang out," Asher said. "One of our first concerts was here. They've always been super supportive of us. They have great taste." He smiled over the top of his mug. "And good coffee."

"They like to claim the whole band is from here," Zeke said. "So does Sydney. If one of us is from somewhere, the whole place will try to claim all of us. It's funny as fuck."

That was normal. Australia was often trying to claim people from New Zealand as ours too. Vice versa, probably.

"Whatever it is, they were really great last night," I said.

Either the people in Melbourne didn't read tabloids, or they were just nicer to me than the Sydney crowd. That wasn't to say I hadn't encountered my share of the press here too. A contingent waited outside the venue for us to go past and several threw questions at me. One or two were related to my singing. The rest were about Vance and my affair with Pete.

I ignored all of them, lifted my chin and stepped into the venue surrounded by six hulking rock stars. It was the best, 'fuck you,' I could give them without words.

The photos of us which later showed up online were a hot-blooded woman's fantasy right there. If only they knew how much of that fantasy I was really living. On the other hand, fuck them. They didn't need to know how lucky I was.

"They'll be really great tonight too," Zeke said. "The fans who went last night have been raving on social media all day. Tonight's crowd will be even more psyched up."

"Especially the ones who went last night as well," Asher said. "And the other night in Sydney. There are whole social media pages of people who follow us all around the country whenever we tour. I can't decide if it's cool or if they're stalkers."

"I think it's cool," I said. It was pretty fucking awesome to have fans that dedicated.

"Stalkers wouldn't pay for tickets, would they?" I grimaced. "Wait a minute, I don't want to know." They'd probably do whatever it took to get close to the object of their affection. No one ever said they acted rationally.

Honestly, I didn't want to think about it too much. I had enough trouble without throwing stalkers into the mix.

"I think it depends on the stalker," Asher said. "I mean, if I was going to stalk me I would spend my money on tickets."

"Me too," Tully said. "We might have enough tickets on ourselves as it is, though."

"Speak for yourself," Asher retorted. "I'm humble."

"No offence, dude, but you just said you would spend a lot of money buying tickets to see yourself," Zeke said. "That doesn't sound very humble to me. It sounds pretty fucking awesome though. I'd buy tickets to see you too."

"I'd buy tickets to see U2," Tully said. "They're my second favourite band after us. Is there a better song than 'I Still Haven't Found What I'm Looking For'?

When I was younger, I dreamt of playing with Bono."

"Who didn't, bro?" Asher asked.

"I didn't," Penn said.

Everyone turned to look at him.

"You didn't?" Tully asked.

Penn shrugged. "I wanted to be successful because of my own talent and hard work, not because I was riding on someone else's coattails. Or fucking them." Of course he couldn't resist giving me the side eye.

"Piss off," I growled. Just because I wasn't quite as skilled at the keyboard as him...

"All of us are successful because of our talent and hard work," Zeke said, speaking over Penn's response. "Even me." Of course he couldn't resist a dig at himself to lighten the mood.

I tilted my head at him. Even joking, I hated hearing people put themselves down. Especially someone as awesome as Zeke.

"No one could ever accuse you of not being talented," I said firmly. "For some reason, it seems to be easier to accept that a man can be successful without having to suck anyone off." I glared at Penn. His words got under my skin much more than I should have let them.

I pushed my empty coffee cup aside and got to my feet. "Excuse me, I need some air."

I waved Zeke and Asher back down when they both started to stand. "I'm fine. I just need a moment."

Neither of them looked happy about it. Nor did Tully for that matter, but they all stayed in their seats while I slipped out the door and into the street.

Not wanting to see three worried faces, and Penn's smug one, in the window, I turned and headed off in the other direction.

Channing and Landon went to do some sight-seeing and shopping, so I kept an eye out for them just in case. In my current mood, I didn't want to answer any more questions and no doubt they would have them.

I pulled a pair of sunglasses out of my bag and slipped them on my face. I should have a hat so I didn't get sunburnt, but in my experience that was the easiest way to draw attention to myself.

Something about the combination of hat and sunglasses screamed, 'I'm trying to hide my identity.' If I wanted to keep from being noticed, I had to act casually. I was just another person going about their day in the city.

That illusion lasted for all of about five minutes,

before a young woman glanced at me, looked away, then looked back. She whispered to her friends, who all started to stare.

"It is, isn't it?" one whispered loudly.

"It looks like her," another said. "She *is* on tour with Wolf Venom."

Fuck.

I gave them a smile and hoped they would keep on walking.

Of course, they didn't. All four of them hurried up to me, phones in their hands.

"Abbie Hart?" one asked tentatively. She had bright red hair and more freckles than I could count.

"Guilty," I said, trying not to sigh. "Hello there."

A woman with dark hair in a mess of curls squealed. "I told you guys!"

The redhead winced. "Amber! I'm pretty sure they heard you in Tasmania."

Amber looked unapologetic. "Can we get a selfie?"

"Sure." Even before everything turned to shit, I never said no to a fan who wanted a selfie or an autograph. What was a couple of minutes out of my day to make their day better?

She posed beside me and held up her phone.

I slipped off my sunglasses and smiled. "Say cheese."

She took a picture of us smiling and one of us laughing at the absurdity of saying cheese.

"Can I have one too?" the redhead asked.

I posed with all four of them in turn and then with the five of us together. They all took turns in taking a photo of us as a group.

"Thank you so much," Amber gushed. "You've been so sweet. We've all been fans since your first album, haven't we girls?"

"Yes we have," the redhead said. "We can't wait for the show tonight."

I had a funny feeling they were big fans of Wolf Venom, but were aware of my music from before I signed with White Wolf Records. At any rate, they were being nice, so the least I could do was be nice in return.

"You're going to have the time of your life," I assured them. "Blazing Violet and Wolf Venom are both on fire right now." If only they knew at least four of the guys were a couple of hundred metres away. They would absolutely lose their minds.

They all looked like they were ready to jump up and down with excitement.

"We should let you go," the redhead said finally.

"No doubt you have a shit load of things to do before tonight. We do. We came in to get our nails done and buy new outfits."

"I'm sure you'll look amazing," I said. "I'll keep an eye out for you."

"We'll be waving like crazy," Amber said.

"I'll wave back," I assured her. The four of them would probably make it up near the front somehow. "Enjoy the rest of your day."

"You too." To my surprise, each of them gave me a quick hug before they hurried on, talking excitedly.

It was a refreshing change from Penn's accusation that I was riding on the band's coattails. I hurt my own feelings by remembering his comment. Mostly, it stung because it was in the back of my mind from the moment I signed with White Wolf Records.

When Jackson suggested I go on tour with the guys, I almost said no because of it. I wanted to stand on my own two feet. I still did.

As for the press, I could just imagine what they would say if they knew about my growing relationship with the guys. They wouldn't pull any punches. They would say any success I had from here on out was because of who I was fucking.

The question was, how did I get past that? I didn't

want to stop being with the guys and I didn't want to flush my career back down the toilet just when it was starting to climb back out.

How in the hell was I going to have everything I wanted and needed without looking like an idiot?

I slipped my sunglasses back on and ignored the looks from a few people who sat at tables at a nearby café. They must have witnessed the exchange with the four other women and all the fuss they made over me. At a quick glance, I didn't think any of them knew who I was. Not to look at me anyway. My name tended to be more recognisable than my face these days.

Again, I wondered if I should colour my hair bright blue. Fewer people would recognise me that way. Until they saw me at a concert with bright blue hair, then I would stand out like dog's balls. Okay, that might be a bad idea.

In the past, when things were at their worst, I'd taken to wearing a brunette wig. It only fooled the press for a little while and led to rumours that I wasn't a natural blond.

It was strange the things they decided to focus on and target me for. As if anyone really cared what my natural hair colour was. Well, unless they want to be an Abbie Hart lookalike. That actually happened more often than you might think.

"Hey, wait up," a voice called out behind me.

I didn't need to turn around to know it was Asher.

He and the other three guys caught up to me, and Asher slid his hand into mine.

"Are you doing okay?" Zeke asked. "Penn can be a dickhead sometimes, but his bark is worse than his bite. Right, Penn?"

"My bite is fucking awesome," Penn said. "Zeke wants me to say sorry, but I'm calling it how I see it. How plenty of other people see it. It is what it is."

I tried to stop myself, but I couldn't help it. I rounded on him so fast he took a step back.

"You don't think I fucking realise that?" I snarled. "I know what people are thinking and saying, because I'm thinking it myself. This was your tour and I should have said no to coming along. This whole fucking thing was a giant mistake."

I threw up my hands and glared through a haze of tears. "People are paying to see *you*. Not me. I should be back in Sydney working on my new album and planning my own fucking tour. Are you happy now? Or would you prefer I just packed up and went home?"

"As a matter of fact—" he started.

"Abbie, no," Asher said. "Penn, what the fuck?"

"No one's going home," Zeke said.

Without meaning to, I snapped at him, "Maybe they are."

I turned and stalked away in the direction of our hotel. The small glimmer of happiness I got from meeting those fans was shattered into a thousand pieces already. All I wanted to do was be as far away from here as possible. From Melbourne, from the guys, especially from Penn.

Until I saw the cardboard box sitting outside the door to my hotel room.

14

ASHER

I GAVE Penn a dirty look and hurried off after Abbie.

It didn't help that he was right, to some extent. Not about Abbie going home. Not when he said she didn't have a place on the tour. No, he was right about people talking, and saying the shitty things he said. He didn't have to regurgitate them, especially the way he had.

There was honesty and then there was being a motherfucker. He definitely crossed that line.

"Abbie, wait," I called after her a couple of times. She didn't wait or even slow, until I skidded to a stop behind her, a couple of metres from the door to the hotel room.

"Fuck. Is that what I think it is?"

She shook her head. "I don't know. It looks like

the one Jonah's head was in. I can't bring myself to look."

She flinched when I put a hand on her shoulder.

"We shouldn't stand out here. Someone might come." I stepped around her and crouched beside the box.

"What the fuck? Not another one." Zeke stopped behind Abbie and placed his hands protectively on her shoulders.

Tully pulled up a couple of seconds later. "What is it—shit."

"Fucking great, more drama," Penn said. "What the fuck next?" He threw up his hands.

"Be glad you're not inside there," I growled. I scooped up the box and waited for someone to pull out a keycard.

"What the shit is that supposed to mean?" Penn demanded.

I ignored him and stepped inside when Zeke unlocked the door.

"Come in or stay out there, but either way close the door," I said to Penn. I placed the box on the table and looked at it for a long moment. "Do we want to guess who is inside this?"

"Yeah," Zeke said sarcastically. "Whoever gets it

right gets a hundred bucks." He exhaled loudly. "Just open the fucking thing. Or I will."

"Be my guest." I waved my hand at the box and took a step back.

To be honest, I was really hoping this time there would be a cake inside there. I mean, a guy could hope, right?

Zeke took his hands from Abbie's shoulders and stepped over to the box. He slipped open the lid and peered inside.

"The bad news is it's not a cake. I also have no idea who it is."

"But it is a who?" I asked tentatively.

"It's definitely a who," he agreed.

Abbie groaned.

Tully placed a hand lightly on her lower back and started to lead her over to the couch. "Come and sit for a—"

"Wait," Zeke said. "Abbie, you need to look and see if you know who this was." He looked pained, like the last thing he wanted was Abbie anywhere near the box. "Shit, I'm sorry."

She nodded and reluctantly walked the few steps back to glance inside the box.

"Fucking hell," she said softly.

"You know who it is?" I asked as gently as I could,

considering we were talking about another disembodied head.

"Yeah, she was Pete's wife," she said in a tiny voice.

"The woman who wanted you kicked off your label when she got back together with him?" Zeke asked.

Abbie nodded and leaned into Tully. "I hated her guts, but I didn't want this to happen to her." After a moment, her eyes snapped up to Zeke's face. "What are we going to do? Should we tell the police?" She looked terrified.

"Fuck no," he said. "We'll deal with this." He looked over at me and I nodded.

"I'll contact my sister. She'll know someone." I pulled out my phone and tapped an innocent looking message into the screen before pressing send.

"You have a brother who lives in Melbourne, don't you?" Abbie asked Zeke.

"Yeah, I do, but he would go straight to Reuben about this." Zeke closed the lid on the box. "The last thing we need to do is give him more ammunition. If they pin this on any of us, the tour and the band are fucked. Even if the allegation doesn't stick, which it wouldn't, we'd be in enough trouble for our careers to be over."

I smiled.

"What?" Penn snapped.

"You've met my sister, Rose," I said. "If anyone can find a way to pin this woman's disappearance on her husband, it will be her."

Zeke smiled. "I like that idea. Get us out of the shit and get some revenge for Abbie in the meantime." We exchanged high-fives.

"You guys are completely insane," Penn said. He sighed dramatically out his nose. "You're going to make me take part in this, aren't you?"

"Sorry, Penny, you're already in this as deep as the rest of us are," I said without even a hint of apology. He deserved it after being an asshole. "If it was you in trouble, we would help you out, and you know it. We have in the past."

He hated discussing that time in his life, but I couldn't help bringing it up right now. I was pissed off at him for what he said to Abbie. I still hadn't ruled out the idea of punching him in the cock, or the face. Maybe when this was dealt with.

He crossed his arms over his chest and scowled. "Fine. If only to make sure it's dealt with."

"Tully?" I asked.

"I'm in," he said immediately.

"We're in too," Landon said as he and Channing stepped through the door. "What are we in— oh. Is that another one of those gifts?"

They both had arms full of bags, Landon maybe double as many as Channing. They set them down beside the door. It looked like they had a successful shopping trip.

"If you want to call it that," Zeke said.

My phone pinged. I pulled it out and looked at the screen.

"Rose says to head on over. We'll have to borrow one of the tour vans. It's going to be a squeeze." I went to pick up the box.

"Wait a minute, you fucking idiot," Penn said. "If that's the same kind of box the others were found in, don't you think someone is going to notice?"

I hesitated, my hands a few centimetres from the box. "You're right. We need something a rock band would carry around without looking strange."

Zeke nodded. "Tully and I will go to the venue and grab a box out of the rig truck. There must be hundreds they used to carry around our equipment. The rest of you stay here and don't answer the door to any police or press."

I nodded, locked the door behind them, and walked over to the bench in the corner of the room.

I flicked on the kettle that sat in the middle of a tray, and started to make us all coffee.

We weren't far from the venue, but it was still going to take some time. Time in which none of us was going to relax. It wasn't too much of a stretch to think whoever left the head might have informed someone about its existence.

The longer the minutes ticked past, the more nervous I got.

Abbie looked even more anxious than I felt. I wanted to hold her and tell her this was all going to be okay, but was it?

If anyone was going to be screwed over in this, it was her. I was going to do everything I could to make sure that didn't happen.

Hell, I was going to find a way to make whoever the fuck was doing this, pay.

I was only ready to admit this to myself for now, but I was in love with Abbie. I was not going to let anything bad happen to her. I was sure as hell not going to let anyone pin the blame for this on her.

I jumped at a tap on the door and cold coffee splashed over my hand.

I hadn't realised I'd stood there lost in thought for over half an hour. None of us had said a word since Tully and Zeke left. I hadn't even taken a sip of my drink.

I put my cup aside, shook my hand to dry it, and stepped over to the door.

"Who is it?" I called out. *God, don't let it be the police. Or anyone from the label. Or a roadie. Or a fan. Or...*

"It's Tull and I. Let us in," Zeke said.

I exhaled in relief and unlocked the door. I opened it a crack and peered out to make sure it was only Zeke and Tully, then opened the door and stepped back. Between them they carried a box big enough for one of Channing's saxophones.

Tully kicked the door closed behind him and they opened the box.

"Bring that over here." Zeke waved at the cardboard box.

We all looked at it, but I was the one who moved to pick it up and place it inside the other box.

I wasn't sure if it started to smell or if I was imagining it, but I moved quickly with it anyway. I wasn't squeamish, and I'd seen dead people before, but the whole situation was different. Nastier somehow.

"If anyone asks, we're taking an instrument to be fixed," Zeke said. "The mouthpiece got broken. Channing got too rough with it, or something."

"Wouldn't happen," Channing said. He didn't look too worried about the false accusation though. It was for a good cause after all.

"Maybe you hit Penn with it," I said dryly.

Penn flipped me off. "Maybe he tried to beat some sense into Asher."

"Okay, quit it," Zeke snapped. He and Tully closed the saxophone box and he hefted it into his arms. "Asher, in my pocket are keys to the van."

"Is that all that's in your pocket?" I reached inside and pulled out the keys.

Zeke chuckled. "No, that's not all. But that's all that matters right now. All of you stay close to me and Abbie. But… try to look like we're not up to something."

That was going to be a stretch since we were *definitely* up to something.

I opened the door and held it while Zeke carried the box out. The rest of us did as he asked and stayed close to Abbie. I slipped my arm around her waist and pulled her hip to mine, but she looked pale and scared.

"We've got this," I assured her. "This isn't the first time we've dealt with shit like this. It's probably not even the tenth."

"But is it the last?" she asked. "Or is this the third in a long line of shit like this? What if it never ends?"

"I hate to say it," Penn said slowly, "but even you are going to run out of people who hate you sooner or later. This bitch and that Vance asshole were the two worst, weren't they? Who else is there? And don't say me, because no one is cutting off my head."

Abbie shrugged. "Pete. Poppy Newton. I'm not sure either of them hate me, they just made my life difficult. Honestly, I don't think Vance and Calista hated me either, so you're probably safe." She gave him a sarcastic half smile.

He sneered at her in return.

Yep, in spite of all the words and dirty looks, they were still hot for each other. It was only a matter of time before they gave in. It was probably even less time before she and Tully became more involved. He was quickly becoming a fourth wheel in this arrangement. In a good way.

We followed Zeke to the van and piled inside, the box safely in the back.

I took the driver's seat with Zeke beside me. The others took the two rows of passenger seats in the back.

"I hope Rose knows what you're getting her into," Zeke said.

"Nothing she can't handle," I said. She was one of the toughest women I knew. She and Abbie would get along.

I hoped.

Rose had a tendency to make snap judgements and stick to them for life.

I started the engine and we headed out to the suburbs.

With any luck, we'd be back before anyone noticed we weren't around. Not to mention back in time for tonight's concert. Missing that would get us into more trouble than being found with a severed head.

Well, almost.

15

ASHER

"How nice of you to drop by with a present," Rose said dryly.

She lived in an unassuming townhouse in Carlton. It reminded me of Zeke's place, but bigger, and decorated with a lot more pastels colours and floral patterns. We always joked that she had taken her name and ran with it.

I guessed you could say that about most of the family.

Dane was like a Great Dane, growling and snarling while trying to protect us. Me, I was trying to set the world on fire, figuratively speaking. The only one who deviated was Mina. She didn't have a mean bone in her body. At least she didn't compared to the rest of us.

I grinned. "You know me, always dropping by with something fun."

Rose peered into the box. "Friend of yours?"

"Yes. I always like to cut the heads of my friends. It stops them from running away." While she rolled her eyes at me, I told her the real story.

She looked over at Abbie with curious eyes. "I heard about you from Dane. He seemed to like you."

Abbie gave her a watery smile. She didn't seem in much of a mood for small talk. "Thanks. He seems nice. Can you deal with that for us?"

"Blunt," Rose said approvingly. "I can, but I might need something in return some day."

"Whatever we can do," I said. "Within reason."

I brushed hair back from Abbie's cheek and stroked the back of my finger along her jaw.

Her skin was still pale from the shock of seeing another disembodied head. It wasn't something anyone should get used to seeing. As chill as I was about it, my stomach still turned being in the same room with it. The whole situation was all kinds of fucked up.

"Yeah, as long as it doesn't involve us getting in the middle of shit between my family and the Bells," Zeke said. "Or the Fiorellis, for that matter."

"I make no promises," Rose said. "Dane has put us

in a precarious position. Men and their cocks." She looked at Abbie and rolled her eyes.

Abbie responded with a half smile. "Men and their ambition."

"I feel attacked," I said dryly.

"Me too," Zeke said. "Sounds pretty accurate though."

"Well... Yeah." I shrugged.

"Can we get this over with?" Penn said.

"Still got the stick up his ass I see," Rose remarked. Before he could respond, she added, "I will deal with the head. You mentioned you wanted the finger pointed at this Pete guy, if possible? Was that Vance person with his label too?"

"Yes, he was," Abbie said. "Why?"

"Two people turned up dead and they're connected to the same person," Rose said slowly. "Is it possible Pete is actually involved?"

Abbie sucked in a breath. "I hadn't even thought of that. I don't think so, but... I mean, maybe."

"Are you suggesting he killed all these people and is trying to pin it on Abbie?" Tully asked. "What an asshole."

"I'm only saying it's possible." Rose tapped the tips of her long, bright red fingernails against her cheek. "The question is, what would be less disruptive, if this head turned up on his doorstep, or if she disappeared entirely? This could turn up in six months time. Twelve months. Or never. Any idea where the rest of her is?"

I shook my head. "None. That could be a problem, couldn't it? Bits of her might start to turn up sooner or later."

"Yeah, but there's nothing we can do about that," Rose said.

"If her head turns up in the next day or two, people are going to ask Abbie questions," Zeke said. "People are going to notice because she is connected to this woman and Vance as well. Even if we can prove where Abbie was when Calista was killed, it's still going to cause a stir. Personally, I'd prefer to avoid a stir of this kind."

"Me too," Abbie said. "If it interferes with the tour—"

"You could always drop out," Penn said.

"Give it a fucking rest," I snarled. "If nothing else, she is under contract, and Levi isn't going to tear it up. Get the fuck over it."

Penn rolled his eyes and stalked away toward the townhouse's pretty courtyard.

"So, disappearing this for a while," Rose concluded. "We wouldn't want anything like a mere murder to get in the way of your careers." Her tone was somewhere between amused and ironic.

"We really wouldn't," I agreed. "You're the best, sis."

"Of course I am," she said. "I'm wondering if I should make Dane disappear as well, before we all end up in trouble."

I laughed. At least, I thought she was joking.

She raised an eyebrow at me.

My smile faded. "Anyway, we appreciate this. I know it's not the best present I've ever brought along with me."

"It's not the worst either," she said. "There was that cake that time."

I sighed. "How many times do I have to say sorry? I had no idea there were nuts in it. Lucky you keep an EpiPen handy."

"That's not by luck," she said dryly. "It's because I don't want to die by being poisoned by my baby brother."

I clapped a hand to my forehead. "Well at least a head in a cardboard box can't poison you. Unless you eat it." I lowered my hand slowly. "You're not going to eat it, are you?"

She might have a particularly unorthodox way of disposing of remains that I didn't know about. I made a note not to eat any meat products she offered me ever again.

She socked me hard on the arm. "No, I'm not going to eat it, you fucking idiot. Did you hit your head with the drumsticks a few times too many?"

I stuck my tongue out at her. "You *were* my favourite sister."

"Only because Mina doesn't talk to you anymore." A shadow passed across her eyes.

"I miss her too," I said softly.

Abbie leaned against me and gave me a squeeze. "She sounds a special person."

"She was," I said. "She *is*. I respect her need to cut the rest of us out of her life, but it still sucks."

"At least I'm still talking to you," Rose said. "In spite of the dubious gifts you bring me. How about some books next time? Or a voucher for one of those nice gardening places. Or home decor places. Or even a nice bottle of expensive wine."

"Well I'm sorted for the next five birthdays and Christmases," I said lightly. "I won't need to ask you what you want."

"You should still ask," she said. "I might have changed my mind by then."

I groaned. "So is there anything you want us to

do? Turn on the barbecue? Dig a hole? To get rid of the head I mean."

She shook her head. "No, I'll deal with it. The less you know about it the better. If people start asking questions, you don't want to have the answers to them."

"We've had a lot of practice in lying," I said. "But you're right, it's a lot easier if we don't know anything."

"I'm always right," Rose said. "One day you'll remember that." She wagged a finger at me.

I swatted it away playfully. Yeah, I'd much rather deal with my relatives than Zeke's.

"We're sorry to get you involved in this," Abbie said softly. "I don't know what I would have done if I had to deal with it by myself."

"You would have figured something out," I said confidently.

Chances were, her career would have been over the moment Jonah's head turned up.

Or worse. Without Zeke to stop her, she would have gone straight to the police. If she told them about Jonah and the gun, Reuben would have had her killed. She wouldn't have walked out of the police station alive. Or if she had, she wouldn't be alive long after that.

Sometimes knowing dubious people like us was an advantage.

"I would have been fucked and you know it," Abbie said.

I grinned.

She smacked me on the chest. "I didn't mean that kind of fucked."

"I know, I couldn't resist." I rubbed my chest. If I wasn't careful, these women were going to leave bruises.

"Try harder," Rose said. "I don't need to know about your sex life."

"Right back at you, sis," I said. Honestly, I had no idea if she even had one. Most men seemed to be scared of her for some reason. Oh, it might be because her baby brother was a big, badass rock god. That would do it, right?

Yeah, okay, maybe it was because she was scary. She took no bullshit from anyone, and was smart enough to figure out a way to pin this on Pete without causing Abbie and the rest of us too much drama.

"Are you expecting a guest?" Channing said from the front of the townhouse. He and Landon were assigned to keep watch, just in case someone spotted us.

"No," Rose said. "Just you clowns."

"Well, a black SUV just pulled up outside the front. I can't see inside, but I have a feeling they're watching this place." Channing shrugged.

"Fuck," Zeke said under his breath. "If you can take care of this, I'll go and see who it is."

"Go for it." Rose picked up the box and carried it to the back of the house.

I had no idea exactly what she'd do with it, but if the police arrived and searched the place, I was sure they wouldn't find it. She was way too smart for that.

I followed Zeke to the front of the house, my arm still around Abbie. I leaned around the curtain and looked out the window.

The SUV was just as Channing described. It reminded me of the one that followed us around that night in Sydney.

"This is just a wild guess here, but I would say Reuben is probably involved," I said.

"I'd say you're right," Zeke said. "Tully, Channing, Landon: keep an eye on Abbie. Asher, you and I are going to go and talk to them."

"Are you sure that's a good idea?" I glanced around to see Penn come in from the courtyard.

"Who's doing something stupid now?" he asked.

"Wanna come and find out?" I asked him.

He shrugged. "Sure. It could only get me killed, right?"

I patted him on the shoulder. "That's the spirit."

He jerked his shoulder away, but followed Zeke and I out the front door and across the footpath.

Zeke walked around to the driver's side window and tapped on it.

At first, I thought whoever was inside was going to ignore us.

Slowly, the window started to slide down.

"I'm not gonna lie, I was hoping it would be someone cool," I said. "Like Levi Jones or the lead singer of the Rock Dragons, what is his name? Strike West? Yeah, that's it."

Stuart 'Strike' West was a legend.

Zeke grinned. "That would be cool."

"Their keyboard player is cooler," Penn said.

"You always think the keyboard player is cooler," I remarked.

"That's because they are." He looked through the car window. "What the fuck is this about?"

The man who sat in the driver's seat looked at us with narrowed eyes. "When you're done with your comedy act, I have a message for you. Specifically for Zeke."

Zeke sighed. "Let me guess, Caleb wishes us well

for our coming tour. Tell him we said thank you very much, it's going nicely so far."

"He wants to see you," the man said.

"Of course he does," Zeke said. "Tell him we're busy. If he wants to talk to me, he's going to have to come to the stadium tonight."

Penn snorted. "Good luck getting past security."

I jerked a thumb toward him. "What he said."

"How did he know we're here?" Zeke asked.

That was a very good fucking question.

The man didn't answer. Instead, he said, "Caleb will see you at the venue before the concert. Have security informed so there's no trouble." The window slid back up and he drove away.

"That's fucking great," Zeke growled. He looked ready to punch someone. Or something. "When will my motherfucking family learn how to use text messages?"

I didn't know the answer to that.

Mine knew how to text, but they still pulled shit like this.

16

ABBIE

I NIBBLED on the corner of a sandwich.

I hadn't had much of an appetite since seeing Calista's head in the box. Every time I closed my eyes, all I saw was her hair, damp with her own blood. Thankfully, her eyes and mouth were closed.

However she died, she looked peaceful. As peaceful as she could be under the circumstances.

I hadn't wanted her dead, but I certainly didn't want her to suffer. I didn't want anyone to suffer, not even Vance. Not even Penn when he was being a dickhead. Not even the guys' families when they were making life more difficult.

"What do you think Zeke's brother wants to talk about?" I asked Tully and Asher.

Ever since we arrived at Rod Laver Arena to get

ready for the concert, at least two of the guys had been with me. First it was Zeke and Penn, but they'd swapped out about half an hour ago. Before those two, Landon and Channing had taken a turn.

I felt as though I was walking around with a contingent of bodyguards. Hot, tattooed, talented bodyguards. None of them seemed to mind the duty, even Penn, surprisingly enough. I had a feeling he wanted to fuck with Zeke's brothers. That made a pleasant change from him trying to mess with me.

"Who knows?" Asher said. "Probably the same shit as Reuben. Caleb is funny though because he always has a different angle. Funny weird, I mean. Not funny, ha-ha."

"What do you mean?" I couldn't imagine any of Zeke's relatives being humorous. Okay, maybe the twins, but not Reuben and not Caleb from what I'd heard about him. Zeke must be the only truly funny one in the family. Luckily, he more than made up for the rest of them.

"Like he'll suggest Zeke might help out here and there, and make it like it's no big deal, but every little thing turns into something much bigger. We can get a lot of things past customs as part of the tour, for example. He'll suggest we carry one little case of diamonds, but it ends up being a huge case full of guns or something. There's only so much Jackson can turn a blind eye to. You know?"

"So don't offer to carry anything for any of Zeke's brothers," I said. "Got it." That was a pretty good general rule about anyone's brothers, even mine.

"Speaking of brothers," Tully said softly.

I looked over to the door as Zeke walked in with an older man who looked like a slender version of him. With a lot fewer tattoos, as far as I could see.

"I don't know what's more shocking," Zeke was saying. "The fact you're at a rock concert or the fact you're actually dressed for it. I didn't know you owned a pair of jeans."

They were black jeans at that, paired with a dark button down shirt. I would have called Caleb hot if I hadn't seen Zeke first.

Like the rest of the family, he had that air of danger about him. That wasn't from just having learned he ran guns and smuggled diamonds either. He looked as though he'd be more comfortable telling someone to kill someone else than he would ordering a fast food meal. Or attending a rock concert for that matter.

"I own several pairs," Caleb said evenly. "I even listen to music once in a while."

"You're shitting me?" Zeke said sardonically. "Next you'll be telling me you smile once in a while."

Caleb did smile. He even laughed, which sounded sexier than it probably should. "I'm not Reuben. I know how to have a good time once in a while."

"Yeah?" Zeke asked. "When? When you're rocking out in the front row of a Wolf Venom concert? Or when you're trying to set me up to get in the shit?"

"Both of those are fun," Caleb said. "Would you believe I'm just here to say hello to my younger brother?"

Zeke responded to that with a flat stare. "No."

Caleb shrugged. "Suit yourself." He seemed to notice the rest of us standing on the other side of the room for the first time. He gave nods to Tully and Asher, which weren't quite warm, but also weren't as chilly as the look Reuben would have given them. His eyes lingered on me, curious and admiring.

In about three seconds flat, he had me mentally naked and standing in front of him. Or kneeling, since his eyes settled on my mouth.

I swear I saw his cock twitch in his pants.

"This is—" Zeke raised his arm to gesture towards me.

"I know who she is," Caleb interrupted. "Abbie

Hart. You're quite an interesting woman from what I've heard."

If he was trying to intimidate me, it wasn't going to work.

"I absolutely am," I said with no hint of modesty. "I'd hate to be boring. Where would the fun be in that?" I smiled sweetly.

"I have no idea," he replied. "Personally, I try not to be boring as well." He licked his lips like a hungry wolf.

Zeke cleared his throat. "Why don't you tell us why you're really here, so then we won't waste any more of your time?" He looked like he was about ready to pick up Caleb and throw him through the nearest window. Was he big enough to do that? He looked angry enough.

"You can also tell us how you knew we were at my sister's place," Asher said.

"Lucky guess," Caleb shot back.

"Bullshit," Zeke snapped. "Someone in the crew is working for you. Who is it?"

Caleb turned towards him slowly. "If they were, why would I tell you? That would be fucking stupid. Exactly how long would it take before you had them fired?"

"About two seconds," Zeke said. "I don't appreciate having people watch me and spy on me for you or for Reuben. I'm not a twelve-year-old. If you won't tell me, I'll find out for myself." His eyes snapped with anger.

"For the record, no one is working for me." Caleb was completely unruffled. "I can't guarantee they aren't working for Reuben and feeding me information."

"It's the same. Fucking. Thing," Zeke snarled.

"How closely are they watching?" I didn't know I was going to speak until the words were out, but there they were. I couldn't take them back.

"Close enough that I know you, my brother and Asher are having a relationship with each other." What Caleb thought of that, I couldn't tell.

I would do as well playing poker against him as I would against Reuben. Badly. I made a note never to play strip poker with any of them.

"Close enough to see anyone delivering any presents to any of us?" Asher asked.

"Zeke, your brother is—" Landon skidded to a stop at the doorway. Channing was right behind him, and almost ran into his back.

"I see he found you," Landon said as he ducked aside to avoid getting bowled over.

"I told you Caleb would find him." Penn appeared

half a minute behind the other two. "I don't know if he's got a radar or if he's one of those dogs that sniffs out shit."

Apparently he had no filter when it came to Caleb either.

"If I was the kind of dog that sniffed out drugs—" Caleb started.

Penn's face turned pink and his lip curled.

"Can you tell us what you're fucking here for?" Zeke snapped.

I had a feeling if Caleb didn't hurry up, Penn was going to pick up something heavy and use it on him. That wouldn't end well for any of us, especially Caleb.

"I'm here looking out for one of the family's assets," Caleb said as if that couldn't be construed as offensive at all.

Zeke gave him a hard stare. "Are you talking about me? I am not a motherfucking *asset.*"

"That was what I tried to tell Reuben," Caleb said. "But if you're not an asset, then you're a liability. You know what happens to liabilities."

Zeke growled low in the back of his throat and lunged at Caleb. He grabbed the collar of his shirt, drove him back and pinned him to the wall.

"*Don't fucking come here and threaten me.* You

might have contacts but so do I. If you don't leave me, my band and Abbie alone, I will fucking *end you*. Do you hear me?"

He shoved Caleb a little harder. Any more pressure and he'd put his brother through the wall.

"Get your hands off me," Caleb said coldly. He sounded a lot more composed than I would be if I was in his shoes.

Zeke held him there for a good minute or two more, then stepped back.

"Get the fuck out of here before I have security throw you out on your ass."

I had no doubt he could and would do just that. Honestly, I wouldn't blame him. Coming here to threaten him took some balls, but it was a dick move on Caleb's part.

I had a funny feeling he wouldn't care very much about my opinion.

Caleb straightened his shirt and stepped away from the wall. His gaze swung around to me. "When you get tired of playing with boys, look me up. I'll show you how real men fuck."

"Um, thanks." What else was I supposed to say to an offer like that? He seemed to be completely sincere in the offer as well. Of course, he was out of his tree if he thought I would actually take him up on it. He wasn't even in the ballpark when it came to being as hot as any of the Wolf Venom guys.

He nodded and strolled out the door as though completely un-worried and unhurried.

"Well, he's a fucker," Penn remarked. "To be honest, I've always thought so."

"I've never known you to be anything other than honest," Zeke told him. "You're a hundred percent right, he is a fucker."

"I see what you mean," I told Asher. "He seemed like he was trying to be nice and then, bam." I could hardly believe he'd blatantly threatened Zeke the way he had. Maybe I shouldn't be surprised, given the kind of people these were.

"Yeah, his family doesn't really do nice," Asher said. "They do pretend nice and then they threaten to kill you."

I stepped over to Zeke and wound my arms around his neck. He was so tense and stiff with anger. I wanted to soothe it away if I could.

"Would they really do that?" I asked softly. "Try to kill you?"

He put his arms around me and rested his head on my shoulder. "They might if they realised I'm never going to give in and go back. They can try though, but they're not gonna succeed. I meant what

I said to him. I also have contacts. We're talking last resort shit here, but I'll do what I have to do to keep myself and all of you safe."

Asher stepped to the side of us and put his arms around us both. "I'll do whatever I have to do too."

Tully slipped over to the other side and also embraced us. "Me too."

"I'm always up for a group hug," Landon said.

"I am too," Channing agreed.

They both surrounded us and gave us all a big squeeze.

On some unseen signal, we all turned and looked over to Penn.

"What?" He sighed through his nose. "Fine. Whatever happens, I'm in too."

He squashed in between Asher and Landon and somehow we all managed one big hug.

Let them throw things at us. We had each other's backs and nothing was going to tear us apart.

17

ASHER

"Is it wrong that seeing you pin Caleb to the wall was hot?" I grinned over my shoulder at Zeke and stepped into the hotel room.

"It was hot." Abbie kicked off her shoes and pulled the tie out of her hair. She shook her head until it fell to her shoulders, smooth except the kink her tie left behind.

Zeke shrugged and closed the door behind us. "He gave me the shits. He's lucky I didn't shove him through the wall. I was fucking tempted."

"We're rock stars, aren't we supposed to trash rooms?" I asked jokingly.

"Only hotel rooms," Zeke said with a laugh.

"Have you ever trashed a hotel room?" Abbie sat

down on the edge of the bed and started to rub her feet.

"No. That would piss the label off," Zeke said. He pulled off his shirt and threw it over into the corner.

I sat beside Abbie and admired all of his muscles and tattoos. He really was a work of art. They both were.

I turned to her, pushed her back gently and caught one of her feet in my hands. "Let me do that."

She placed her hands behind her head and let out a soft, relaxed sigh. "I'm not going to argue with you. I feel like I've been standing for a week."

"At least the concert went well." Zeke sat beside us wearing only his boxers. He grabbed Abbie's other foot and started to massage her toes.

"When does it not?" She rolled her head to the side to look at him. "Serious question. You guys must have played a bad gig at some point in your lives?"

"The high school talent show was pretty bad." I pressed my thumbs into the arch of her foot. "We played with a bunch of guys who…" I stopped to choose my words carefully. "Let's just say they're not playing music anymore. We were pretty terrible."

"We didn't get chased off the stage." Zeke grinned, looking like a seventeen year kid again.

I chuckled. "That's true. Remember—what was

his name? Orlando? He was trying to juggle and kept dropping the balls everywhere."

Zeke cocked his head at me. "I thought that was the act. He was supposed to drop them and look funny."

I frowned. "Now you mention it, you might be right. I hadn't thought about that."

I rubbed Abbie's toes one by one, then moved up her foot and onto her ankle and calf.

"That feels so good," she groaned.

I grinned and worked my way up higher until I slid my hands up her short skirt and massaged her thigh. Zeke was only a few centimetres behind me.

She raised her hips to undo her skirt and pushed it down. Zeke and I both grabbed the waistband and tugged it down her legs and off over her feet.

She pulled off her own shirt until she lay between us wearing panties and a white, lace bra so sheer, a hint of nipple blushed though.

"If I saw that before the concert, I wouldn't have been able to focus," Zeke said.

"Same here." I kissed the inside of her knee, and slowly licked my way up higher.

Halfway up her thigh, I stopped to pull off my shirt and threw it aside.

I was pleasantly surprised when Zeke unfastened my jeans and helped me out of them.

He must be feeling bolder now. How bold might he get?

I kept on kissing my way up the inside of Abbie's leg, until I was able to run the tip of my tongue over the gusset of her panties.

She shivered deliciously.

I hooked my fingers under the waistband of her panties and slid them down her hips.

"Thank you." Zeke lowered his face between her thighs and teased her pussy with his tongue.

"Any time." I dropped her panties to the floor and scooted up to her side. She twisted her upper body so I could get my hands behind her and unhook her bra. I pulled it down her arms and tossed it over my shoulder.

Then, because fair's fair, I scooted down to help Zeke out of his boxers. His cock was already so hard, I couldn't help but run my tongue over his tip. I watched his face for his reaction. Was it too much, too quickly?

He lifted his glistening mouth off Abbie's pussy and gave me a heated glance.

Not too much then. Shit yeah.

I lowered my mouth onto him, taking as much of

his length as I could fit. I had only done this once before, with a guy whose name I couldn't remember now. I'd thought about doing it to Zeke approximately a bajillion times.

His cock did not disappoint.

Neither did the way he rolled his hips as I sucked and lightly massaged his balls with my fingers. Curious—they felt like mine, but different at the same time. His might be a little longer but mine were wider.

Either way, they felt amazing.

Abbie groaned as Zeke slurped at her pussy. Every sound made my own cock harder and harder, begging to be touched. I could fondle myself, but I waited.

Seeing them both enjoying themselves was even more of a turn on than being touched.

Abbie's hips rolled harder as she cried out as she came.

Was there a more beautiful sound than someone you loved having an orgasm? I couldn't think of one.

Zeke lifted his face and smiled. He was obviously thinking the same thing I was.

"You're overdressed," he told me.

I took my mouth off him and glanced down at my boxers. "So I am." I went back to sucking.

"I hate to interrupt," Abbie said with a laugh. "But I'd like it if one of you would fuck me."

"Asher has a spare cock," Zeke said.

I took my mouth off him again before I choked on a laugh. "You make it sound like I have two of them. I mean, what I have is big enough for two."

Neither of them disagreed with me.

Sweet.

I wriggled out of my underpants and threw them aside.

Zeke gave me a speculative look.

"Whatever you're thinking, the answer is yes," I said immediately.

"You don't know what I'm thinking." He cocked his head and raised an eyebrow. He was so stinking cute.

"I bet I do." I glanced in the direction of the lube which lay on the table beside the bed.

Before he could respond, I straddled Abbie's hips and lowered my mouth to hers in a deep, intense kiss.

"I heard a rumour," I said between kisses, "that you need to be fucked." My cock certainly needed to do some fucking.

"You heard right," she said breathlessly.

"You've come to the right place." I gently pried

her knees apart with mine and pressed my cock into the mouth of her pussy. Even that tiny touch of wet heat was like throwing alcohol onto a raging fire.

With a grunt, I pushed deepinto her.

Her back arched. "Yes, fuck, yes, just like that."

She let out a moan so heady she drove me straight to the edge of the cliff. I had to take a moment and pull myself back before I came too soon. I wanted to savour every second of this. Make it last as close to forever as I could.

Finally, I couldn't hold myself back any longer, I started to pound into her with firm, smooth strokes. "Fuck, you feel good."

In the corner of my eye, I saw Zeke reach for the lube. My heart raced even harder.

It was getting more and more difficult to keep from coming.

It was even more difficult when Zeke placed a tentative, lubricated finger on my rear hole. Lightly, gradually getting more confident, he spread the lube around.

He tossed the tube aside and swallowed audibly.

"Are you sure?" he whispered.

I didn't know if he was checking in with me, himself, or both.

"I'm sure if you are," I told him. "Take your time."

I wanted everything he had to give, but only if he was ready to give it.

"Okay." His voice was rough with desire, laced with a touch of nerves.

Slowly and carefully, he pressed the tip of his finger inside me.

"Is that all right?" He sounded like he would pull it right out at the first sign of my discomfort.

Funny how he could be violent and hot, and then a few hours later sweet, considerate and hot.

I glanced over my shoulder. "It's more than okay, babe. I want…all of you, if you're ready to give it."

I wanted nothing more in the world than to have my cock inside the woman I loved while the man I loved had his cock inside me.

He didn't say anything, but he put his hands on my hips and pressed something hard against my ass. I knew it wasn't any of his fingers, because they were gripping me and trembling slightly.

His cock pressed a little harder, until the tip slid inside me.

I tensed a little and stopped still to let my muscles get used to having him there. Bit by bit, they stretched and relaxed, allowing his thick heat to slip in further.

I thrust into Abbie, then pulled back out and

slowly pushed myself onto him. My muscles stretched more, taking him deeper and deeper.

The sensation of having him inside me, while being seated inside her was like nothing I ever felt before. My balls might explode with how good it felt. It was... The most all encompassing sensation I ever had.

He groaned. "Holy fuck."

Those would have been my words if I was capable of speaking right now. I wasn't, at least not with words. My whole world was all about sliding my cock in and out of Abbie, and feeling Zeke's cock filling me more and more. Finally, he sank all the way into me and started to thrust slowly.

Holy gods. I was ready to see stars a few universes over already.

Leaned forward as I was, I brushed my chest over Abbie's nipples with each stroke. They quickly became hardened peaks, all perky and cute.

I fucking loved her nipples. Hell, I fucking loved all of her.

And all of him.

"You two are killing me," I said. "In the best way possible."

"You're pretty epic yourself," Zeke said. "And so fucking tight."

That sent a shiver of pleasure and delight through me, and made my balls hurt like they might burst.

I was almost certain he'd done anal with plenty of women, so it was nice to know I could hold my own against them. Of course I could, I was me. Or something like that anyway.

I gritted my teeth.

I tried not to come, but when Abbie groaned and came, she forced the orgasm right out of me. I couldn't hold it back any longer.

Almost in harmony we grunted and groaned, driving each other to heights that stole coherent thought and oxygen from my body.

Just when I thought it couldn't get better, Zeke came too, filling my ass with white hot cum.

The grunt of pleasure he gave would have made me come if I wasn't in the middle of an orgasm already. As it was, it lasted longer and ran deeper than ever before.

Almost as one, we sagged and flopped down onto the mattress, cocks sliding out of holes, air sucked back into lungs.

I ended up in the middle of the two most gorgeous people in the face of the planet.

"Are you both good?" I asked once I managed to remember how to speak.

"I am," Abbie said. She stretched her arms above her head.

"Yeah," Zeke said.

He sounded a little... I don't know, off? Not bad, just not quite himself.

I rolled my head to face him. "Are you sure? If that was too soon for you—"

He looked back at me, contemplative rather than upset, thank fuck.

"It wasn't. I just need a minute to get my head around it. I've never screwed another guy before."

I smiled softly, trying to mask the concern I'd pushed him away by moving too fast.

"I'm honoured to be your first."

"I'm glad it was you," he said. "I don't have any regrets, in case that's why you look so worried."

"That obvious, huh?" I should have known he'd see straight through me. He always did.

"I'm glad you don't. I don't either. In fact, I can highly recommend fucking your girlfriend and your boyfriend at the same time."

He grinned. "Hashtag relationship goals."

I grinned back. He might need to work up to doing that, but he seemed willing to try. There were a whole bunch of things I would like to try with both of them, if we could work up to it.

"You know what else is awesome?" Abbie said.

"I turned to face her. "What?"

"If both of your boyfriends fuck you at the same time. But first, I need a shower. Who's with me?"

18

ABBIE

"You'll be fine," Zeke assured me.

I resisted the urge to either look down at my feet or run away.

I might still do both, I hadn't decided yet.

"What if I'm not fine?" I said. "This is a huge deal. If I do this the wrong way, I could end up getting hurt."

Yeah, what was new? These days, I was living my whole life on a knife's edge, a step away from either the end, or something amazing.

"What if Levi Jones wants to see me so he can break the contract?" I asked.

"You've met him before," Asher said. "You know he's a huge fan of yours. The tour has been going perfectly. There is absolutely no reason to think he's going to break anything. If anything, he is probably planning to bring forward the release date of your new album. Strike while the iron is hot and all that."

I groaned. "Don't say that. That fills me with even more anxiety and pressure. It's nowhere near ready. It's going to take months. I'll probably have to rere-cord a lot of it."

Zeke put his hands to either side of my face and turned me to look me in the eye.

"That's bullshit and you know it," he said. "You've made albums before. You could probably do it in your sleep. You know Levi, he would never bring the date forward, or even think about doing it, unless everyone involved was absolutely convinced it was ready. That includes Candy, and I know she's a big fan of yours too. Now, are you going to jump?"

"Yeah, jump. Or get out of the way," Penn said.

I looked down at the water about twenty metres below the rock we stood on. "Are you sure this is a good idea?"

"Of course we do," he said. "We come here every time we're in Queensland. Apart from the concerts, it's the highlight of the tour. This part of it anyway. Would we bring you up here if it wasn't safe?"

"Maybe," I said doubtfully.

All of the guys laughed. Even Penn. To my surprise, he hadn't suggested pushing me off the rock. Yet.

"Okay, but you have to go down with me," I said.

As Zeke grinned. "I'm always happy to go down with you and *on* you." He slipped his hand into mine.

I felt someone take my other hand and turned to see Tully beside me.

"I could use some support too," he said. "I'm scared of heights."

"Really?" I asked. "Big, bad rock god like you?"

He shrugged one shoulder. "Really. We're all afraid of something. Landon is scared of spiders."

Landon shuddered. "Because they're horrible. All those legs wiggling and shit." He wiggled his fingers in the air.

"I don't like small spaces," Channing said.

Asher sighed. "I don't like centipedes. Same thing about wiggly legs. I don't think Zeke is scared of anything."

"I'm scared of accidentally ripping Reuben's head off and living in peace once and for all, but I don't think you'd call it a phobia. More like a fantasy."

I snorted a laugh and glanced sidelong at Penn. I didn't think he would tell me what he was scared of, if he was scared of anything.

He grunted and said, "I fucking hate clowns."

"Yeah, I think that's pretty universal," I said. "They are horrifying."

"Sure are," he said. "Are you gonna jump?"

I sucked in a breath. "Okay, on the count of three?" Zeke and Tully nodded.

"One."

"Two."

"Three."

They both squeezed my hands and we jumped. It felt as though we fell for days, before we plunged through the top of the water and down into the blue depths.

I managed to keep hold of both guys' hands until we bobbed up, laughing and gasping for air.

"That was fun!" I shouted.

"Look out!" Asher shouted. He tucked his arms around his knees as he jumped and landed like a bomb a few metres away.

Water washed over us and I let out a squeal.

"Asshole," I told him when his head appeared above the water.

He grinned. "You know you love me."

He was right, I did. One of these days I would find the right chance to tell him that. Not yet though. I still needed to figure out where I stood with all the other guys and where they stood with each other. Until then, I would be careful not to break their hearts or my own.

I wanted to be absolutely certain about the present, much less the future, before I took any more plunges into deep water.

I adjusted my bikini top, which had somehow managed to stay on even after the jump, and blew him a kiss. He would have to be content with that for now.

I turned and started to swim back towards the beach. Before I got more than about fifty metres, I stopped to watch Penn and then Channing and Landon jump. The bassist and the saxophonist jumped hand in hand, but Penn did a perfect, smooth swan dive.

Of course he had to do it better than everyone else. He always seemed like he had something to prove.

It seemed right to applaud him when he came back up for air.

He gave me a glance, but I couldn't tell if he was pleased or annoyed at the attention.

Rather than stick around and wait for him to scowl at me, I swam back to the beach. I stepped out onto the sand and picked up my towel to wind around myself.

"What is it with Penn?" I asked Tully who had followed me out of the water. The others seemed content to stay in and splash each other, or body surf.

"He always seems to... I don't know, try to be better than everyone else. Like he feels as if he has to try really hard."

Tully picked up his own towel and started to dry his hair. "Uptight upbringing," he said. "His parents had certain expectations. I think he puts those expectations on himself. Or he just wants to be the best version of himself he can be."

"There's nothing wrong with that, I suppose." I sat in the sand, pushed my hat onto my head and pulled out my sunblock. "He could try being a nicer version of himself."

Tully laughed. "There's nothing with trying to be better, unless you drive yourself crazy doing it. You want me to do your back?" He held out his hand and I handed him the sunblock.

I leaned forward while he rubbed it all over my back and shoulders. "Thank you. I'll do yours when you're finished."

Like the rest of the guys, he was tanned, but you

can still get badly burnt even with a tan. I wouldn't be much of a girlfriend or even a friend if I didn't do what I could to stop him from being in pain. Plus, I'd get to touch him with slippery lotion.

Win-win.

"So what are you scared of?" he asked. "Up there on the rock, we all shared our fears. What's yours?" He quickly added, "You don't have to tell me if you don't want to."

"I don't mind," I said. "It's pretty obvious I'm scared of failure, but I don't think that counts. That's kind of an artificial fear brought about by past assholes."

"Totally understandable," he said. "I would also understand a newfound fear of cardboard boxes."

"That too," I winced. "Especially with body parts inside them." I took the bottle from him and scooted around behind him to apply the lotion to his back.

"I'm scared of needles," I said finally. "I know they're necessary at times, but they freak me the fuck out."

"Don't want to sleep for a hundred years?" he asked teasingly.

I snorted. My hand made a wet slapping sound when I lightly socked his back.

"I meant medical needles. I'm also not very fond

of knitting needles, because I have absolutely no finesse for creating things like that. Before you say it, I also don't like pins and needles."

He chuckled. "Who does? Where do you stand on pine needles?"

"I don't mind them, as long as I have shoes on," I said. "Why do I always end up having weird, silly conversations with you guys?"

"Because we're weird and silly?" Tully suggested. "Isn't that what you like about us, or am I stretching here?"

"It's one of the things I like about you," I said. "There are lots of other things too."

"Such as?" he asked.

He was fishing for compliments but I decided to take the bait and let him reel me in.

"I've never felt so included before," I admitted. "I've never felt as much a part of something as I do with you guys. Not just *something*, but something *special*. Also you guys are funny, talented, hot and when I'm around you I feel like a goddess." I couldn't be much more honest than that.

"You are a goddess," he said softly. "I know for a fact we would have found you one way or another. The universe decided it, probably a million years ago. And here you are. That probably sounds even weirder than talking about needles, but I believe we all have a place in the universe and the universe just had to help us find it. Even if it takes a million years."

That was an intense concept. A million years of dust ending up right here on this beach.

"Those are some long-term goals right there," I said. "But I like it. I love the idea that the universe always intended me to find you guys."

"Even Penn?" he asked teasingly. "I shouldn't joke. He is definitely part of the universe's plan for all of us. No one could be given as much talent as he has for no reason. We might not know the reason, maybe ever, but there is one."

"I didn't realise you were so spiritual." I finished his back and put the cap back on the bottle of sunblock.

"I have a variety of interests," he said. "Mostly I'm a big believer in understanding the universe and ourselves. Listening to our bodies, paying attention to what our senses tell us, things like that."

That made sense. We all had times in our lives where we ignored ourselves, whether it was our bodies telling us to slow down, or our instincts telling us not to jump into things.

"Zeke and Asher mentioned you were into..."

How did I even put this? "Blindfolds and things like that," I finished tentatively.

He moved around to sit cross-legged on his towel in front of me. "I'm into increasing what the senses feel, to better appreciate stimuli. Sometimes that includes blindfolds. Sometimes it includes feathers and paddles. It helps to move past the day-to-day and appreciate everything our bodies have to offer us."

He sounded like a meditation guru, but his tone was so casual he could have been talking about last week's cricket match. I'd seen him watching one, so I knew he enjoyed the sport.

After a moment of reflective silence, he added, "Sometimes that also means understanding that pain can bring pleasure. And so can giving pain. Does that scare you?"

"Not nearly as much as needles do," I said. If anything, I was intrigued. Okay, more intrigued than I already was.

"Would you show me some time?" I asked.

He grinned. "Of course I will. I know a place in Perth. I'll take you when we get there, if you like. But I should warn you, it can be a very mind opening experience. Everything might seem boring afterwards."

He wiggled his brows and I got the feeling that was his way of saying he was going to ruin me for all the other guys.

I doubted that, but he was certainly welcome to try.

19

ABBIE

"HEY, I hear things are going good." Levi Jones looked every bit the modern businessman. Long hair tied back in a manbun, worn out jeans and an old T-shirt. He wasn't much older than me but the success of White Wolf Records meant he had a lot more money than I did.

He had a lot more money than all of us. No one could argue he hadn't worked for every cent of it.

"So far," I agreed. The vibe at the weekend long TideFest music event, where Wolf Venom were playing on the Saturday night, was a little strange though. Maybe it was the heat of far North Queensland, or maybe it was my imagination. The crowds seemed a little on edge.

Nothing out of the ordinary happened so far, just

the occasional fight and underage drinking. Security had those in hand before they escalated.

Apart from that, the audience was receptive to Friday night's acts, which had gone on late into the night. When they'd stopped singing, the crowds hadn't. They danced and sang and had a good time until the last of them finally crawled into their tents around dawn.

For the most part, I'd stayed behind the scenes with the guys, hanging out with the other bands and solo acts. I was still fangirling over meeting the legendary Rock Dragons, who had come all the way from the east coast of the United States just for the event.

All of them were so nice and even took selfies with me. Yeah, I felt like a total groupie, except without throwing myself at any of them. From what I could tell, they all had wives or girlfriends anyway, even if I wasn't busy with my guys. If they were the kind to cheat, they weren't my type anyway.

"Thank you for believing in me, Mr Jones," I said sincerely. "I appreciate it so much. I don't even think I can express it."

He grimaced and took a sip of beer straight out of the bottle. "You can start by calling me Levi. Mr Jones makes me sound like I'm sixty years old or something." He smiled to show he wasn't actually offended.

"Levi," I corrected myself. I could relate. I didn't like being called Ms Hart, or Abigail all that much. Both were too formal for me. Better than *washed up bitch*, but still…

"Candy tells me good things about your upcoming record." He waved me toward a couple of camp chairs which were recently vacated by members of Blazing Violet.

I sat and tried not to smile at the quaint way some people in the industry still referred to them as records. Although, lots of albums were still being produced in vinyl record form, the same way some books were produced in hardback. People always liked their collectible forms of art. There was nothing wrong with that.

"I'm pretty sure she could make a singing potato sound good," I said. "Thank you for the vote of confidence though. With her, it's super easy to want to do even better, you know? She gave me a couple of pointers, which made a huge difference."

"If anyone could make a singing potato sound good, it would be her," Levi agreed. "I wish I could find a singing potato. I have a feeling that would make me a rich man." He laughed.

I joined in with him. "I have a feeling you're right. I wonder if they would sing the theme song to MASH."

He laughed even harder. "They probably would, and they'd be good fun at a roast."

I groaned. That was a dad joke worthy of Zeke.

"They'd probably wear skinny jeans and spend all day hashing things out instead of getting boiling mad," he continued. "The only other potato-related pun I can think of is chip, and I can't think how to put that in sentence."

"You could always *not* put it in a sentence," I said with a laugh. "Sometimes you just have to give up when the chips are down."

He put up his hand and I gave him a high five.

"You win that pun-off," he said.

I took a sip from my water bottle. "If I'd known we were having a competition, I would have tried harder."

He looked at me like he was trying to work in another pun, but I was out too, unless I could figure out how to add fry into the conversation.

"Anyway, so far everyone at the label is impressed with you." He leaned back in the chair and crossed his legs like he was sitting in an executive meeting and not in a makeshift backstage area. He looked like he would have been at home just about anywhere.

I envied him that. Would I ever feel that comfortable in my own skin? The guys were certainly going a long way to getting me there, but I still had a long way to go.

"I'm impressed with everyone at the label," I said. "You've brought together such a good team. Everyone is so professional and friendly."

He seemed pleased at the observation. "That was what I was going for. Somewhere relaxed and comfortable, where people are happy to turn up to work each day and work ridiculously long hours. Personally, I can't think of a more rewarding career than working in music. I'm privileged to have had the opportunity to work with people like you and Wolf Venom, the Rock Dragons, and Blazing Violet. The insane amount of talent blows my mind on an hourly basis. You all put your faith in me as much as I put it in you. I am truly honoured and humbled. I know that probably sounds a bunch of bullshit, but it's true."

"It doesn't sound like bullshit to me," I said. "You're right. A good, solid working relationship goes both ways. If you signed the wrong people, your business wouldn't be so successful."

"Exactly," he said. "I've heard some singers who practice a song so much they sound incredible, but if you throw something different at them they sound like a turtle being strangled."

I almost choked on a sip of water. "I hope I don't sound like that."

He grinned. "You wouldn't be here if you did. Unless of course the listening audience wanted that sound. Stranger things have happened." He spread his hands to either side.

"That's true," I said with a laugh. I would never judge anyone for their taste in music, but plenty of it wasn't my thing. Fortunately, most of it was, or I could at least appreciate it for its artistry.

"So, how are the boys treating you?" he asked. "I realised it might have been a big ask to send you on tour with them. They can be a handful. So can their groupies. They tend to gather wherever the guys go." He didn't seem to be concerned or passing judgment, just stating a fact.

"The boys are certainly a handful at times," I agreed.

As for groupies, I noticed them hanging around, especially outside the stage door after concerts. None of the guys seemed remotely interested in any of them. Not even Penn, who had no real reason to turn them down. I had no strings tied to him, even though I wanted to.

"Nothing I haven't been able to handle." I watched his face, trying to gauge his response to my comment. Did he know about my relationships with the guys? Or Zeke and Asher's relationship? Would he care? As long as it didn't interfere with the band, then I couldn't see why he would have a problem with it.

On the other hand, people often had unexpected ideas about things. Levi Jones might be chill, but he was also a businessman. If he thought something would interfere with the label, then he would have something to say about it.

"Good," he said with a nod. "They're an interesting group of boys. Maybe more so than any of my other bands. They've certainly been through a lot."

"So I've heard," I said carefully. "I think everything has brought them closer together. I don't know that I've met another band that got along as well as they do. I mean, they have their moments, like everyone else, but they come together at the end of the day." Sometimes literally.

"What doesn't kill you makes you stronger," Levi said. "You're also proof of that."

"Unfortunately, that's also true," I said. "You heard about what happened to Vance?"

So far, I hadn't heard anything about Calista. At some point, that was going to drop like a bomb. I wasn't looking forward to it. I hoped like fuck Rose would give Asher some warning before it happened so we could brace ourselves. Otherwise, we would just have to weather the storm when it came.

"I did," Levi said. "It couldn't have happened to a bigger piece of shit."

I blinked in surprise. I agreed with him but I hadn't expected him to say that.

"Um. I mean..." I stammered. "It was all very tragic..."

He snorted with absolutely no mercy whatsoever. "I'm sorry for what his family is going through, but if you have to use a talented, beautiful artist because you aren't talented enough to make it on your own, then you're a stone cold asshole. Okay, maybe he didn't deserve to be murdered, but he deserved an ass whipping."

"I can't argue with that," I said with a sigh. "The thing was, he was talented. He was just impatient to get further along in his career."

Levi leaned forward. "If anyone on my label did what he did, I wouldn't just tear up their contract. I would make sure they ended up back where I found them. I have no time for people who step on other people to get their way. This industry is a bitch, and it is difficult to get ahead, I acknowledge that. But if you're going to be a shit person, then you have no business being successful as far as I'm concerned."

He sat back. "I'm sorry, that came off as forceful. I'm a big believer in nurturing talent and letting people grow into their own."

"Some people are saying that sending me on tour with Wolf Venom is a fast track," I said, again speaking carefully. I hoped I wasn't shooting myself in the foot by being so candid.

"That is also bullshit," he said firmly. "You were already on track, you didn't need a shortcut. I wanted you to join this tour to spice things up a bit. Which is exactly what it did. Okay, sure, it give you additional exposure, which is good for you and the label. But no one stepped on anyone else on the way. In fact, it's been good exposure for Wolf Venom as well. And Blazing Violet. I prefer to think of it as a mutually beneficial arrangement."

"I hadn't thought of it that way," I admitted. Now he mentioned it, the extra publicity wouldn't have hurt the guys, it would have helped them. And Violet and her band too.

"That's why I'm the boss," he said with a grin. "It's my job to think of shit like this. Me and my executives. So you guys can make the music and wow the ticket-buying audiences, and we think up ways to get them to part with more and more of their money. It seems to be working pretty well for everyone, I think."

"I think so too," I agreed. "Thank you. I don't mean to sound like an artist with a fragile ego, but it's nice to have some validation once in a while." Not just from the audience, but from someone who put his reputation on the line by signing me after all the shit I had gone through. "You don't regret signing me?"

He looked surprised, but then chuckled. "Not for a second. Not yet anyway. Why? You're not planning to jump ship are you?"

I snorted. "No fucking way. You're stuck with me. Unless I start to sound like a turtle being strangled. Or a singing potato."

"Good, because White Wolf has no plans to let you go any time soon. Even if you're not an actual singing potato." He grinned.

20

ABBIE

"THE CROWD IS TWITCHY," Blaise said as he and the rest of Blazing Violet stepped off the stage. "I don't think they're here to hear us."

In fact, thousands of people who attended the festival, were standing in front of the stage chanting, "Venom! Venom! Venom!"

I peered out through the flats that made up the wings of the stage. "Maybe I shouldn't go out there. It's you guys they want."

Honestly, it sounded like they were ready to tear the place down if they didn't see the guys shortly. *Really* shortly.

Zeke put his hands on my shoulders and started to massage them. "You'll be fine. Go out there, do your thing and they'll settle down."

"They fucking better," Penn growled. "I'm not going out there if they don't. Fuck that."

"Scared of the audience?" Asher asked, teasing lightly.

"Not usually," Penn said. His eyes flicked toward the stage uneasily. "I just don't want to be out there if they start shit."

Neither did I, but when the MC announced me, I sucked in a breath and nodded to myself. I had performed at plenty of events like these before. All I had to do was step out on the stage and sing. Nothing I hadn't done a thousand times before.

"Here goes nothing." I took a step forward, but Asher stopped me. He gave me a quick but searing kiss on the mouth.

"That's for luck. Not that you need it. Go out there and slay them." He patted me on the ass, then gave me a gentle shove out onto the stage.

I turned back long enough to shake my finger at him, then headed over to the microphone. I didn't even get that far before the audience started to boo.

Okay, I was hoping for a warmer reception than that, but I could deal with it. Like Zeke said, I needed to start singing and I would be fine.

I took the microphone out of the stand.

"Get off!" someone shouted.

"Homewrecking bitch!" someone else shouted.

"We want Venom. We want Venom. We want Venom!"

Someone even shouted, "Murderer!"

Fuck. I'd had tough crowds before but this one—

I didn't see anyone throw anything until a sharp pain blossomed through the side of my face and my vision went dim.

"Fuck, get her off the stage!" someone in the crew shouted.

Something warm trickled down my face and someone put an arm around me, but it was all a blur amidst a rain of cans and plastic bottles landing on the stage.

"It's okay, we've got you." That sounded like Zeke's voice. He scooped me up off my feet and carried me off stage to the sound of the audience jeering and shouting insults.

"Fucking hell," Asher said. He crouched beside me as Zeke lowered me to the floor.

I was vaguely aware of him pulling off his shirt and pressing it to the side of my face.

"Someone get the ambos," Zeke said. "And some ice."

"I'm okay," I murmured. I realised that was blood running down my cheek. Someone threw a motherfucking can at my face. A full one, by the feel of it.

"No you're not," Zeke insisted. "I'm no doctor, but you're bleeding."

"Yeah, it looked nasty to me," Asher said.

"I'm not going out on that fucking stage," Penn declared.

"Usually I would suggest you think about someone other than yourself, but in this case I agree with you," Zeke told him. "Is security onto whoever threw that? And the rest of them? Until they've hauled their asses out of here, none of us are going out on stage."

People were talking and running around, but the pain was slowly starting to fade.

"Abbie?" Tully sat beside me and stroked my hair. "You're going to be fine. Think about our date in Perth. We're going to have an amazing time."

"I'm not going to die," I muttered. "It fucking hurts though."

"I know it does," he said soothingly.

"They grabbed the guy," Channing said. He flopped down beside me. "They're dragging him out right now. And a bunch of other people."

"Yeah," Landon agreed. He knelt beside Channing. "It's getting ugly out there. Some people are trying to stop security from dragging them away. They're talking about cancelling the rest of the festival."

"Why do a handful of people have to ruin it for everybody else?" Asher complained. "Most of the crowd was great, it was a handful of people stirring everyone else up."

"Oh my God, what happened?" Violet sounded breathless, as though she'd run back from wherever she and the rest of her band went after their set.

"Assholes started throwing cans and bottles," Zeke growled.

"Fucking hell," that was Levi Jones. He sounded even angrier than Zeke. "Where the fuck are the organisers? I'm going to rip off some heads and—" He stomped away.

I almost felt sorry for the organisers, but if people were out there making trouble, they should have removed them the day before. Honestly, they shouldn't have let me go out on stage if there was that much animosity. I should have listened to my instincts and stayed offstage. If I had, everyone would be rocking out to Wolf Venom right now.

"The ambos are here," Channing said.

"About fucking time," Zeke growled under his breath, although only a couple of minutes had passed. The organisers would have had an ambulance on-site for emergencies and injuries like mine.

The guys, except for Asher—his hand was still on his shirt pressed against my cheek—moved aside to let the ambulance officer crouch down beside me.

"Hi, I'm Dave, what's your name?" He sounded cheerful, like he had done this a million times before. He probably had.

"Abbie," I replied. "It's a Saturday. We are at TideFest."

"No concussion then," Dave said. "I'm gonna take a look at your face. Okay?"

He peeled off the shirt and I winced.

"You have a nasty gash, but I've seen worse." He poked around a little bit. "No need for stitches but I'm going to put a bandage on there to contain the blood and help the skin to knit." He reached around in his bag before cleaning the gash and placing gauze and an adhesive bandage over the top of it.

"Is that going to leave a scar?" Landon asked.

"Are you hoping it will or hoping it won't?" Asher asked.

I was wondering the same thing.

"I dunno," Landon said. "On one hand, scars are cool. On the other hand, Abbie might not want a scar on her face."

I didn't, but I could have had much worse if the can hit a little higher. I could have been knocked unconscious, or worse. Thank fuck they banned glass bottles from events like this. One of those would have hurt like a bitch.

"There you go," Dave said. "Just so you know, I was looking forward to hearing you sing. Big fan. Now, I hate to love you and leave you, but if things get messy out there, I'm going to be needed."

Asher helped me sit up, but I leaned against him because my head spun a little and ached.

"Thank you," I told Dave before he left.

He nodded, rose and hurried away.

Levi reappeared a couple of minutes later. "The organisers are confident they weeded out all of the troublemakers, but they're going to put extra security in the crowd for the rest of the event. It was that or cancel the rest of it." He sucked in a loud, furious breath.

"I refused to let any of you go out there without some sort of measures in place. It's bullshit that it's come to this. People come to these events to enjoy themselves, that includes the fucking acts."

He shook his head in frustration, then crouched beside me. "Are you okay? I'm just about ready to sue the organisers over this. No one should get out there on stage and be the target of projectiles."

"I'm fine," I said quickly. "No need to sue anyone."

He glanced up at Zeke. "They're lucky they didn't throw a bottle at you. They'll be arrested and charged with assault, but at least they'll get out of it alive."

I was wondering if he knew about Zeke and Asher's families, but that comment confirmed it.

"If they threw it at me, I would have picked it up and smashed them over the head with it," Zeke said bluntly. "If I was on stage and saw who did it to Abbie, I would shove it up their ass until it came out their throat."

"You'd have to get in line." Asher said. "I haven't ruled out finding out who they are and doing exactly that."

"Only if you want your contracts torn up," Levi growled. "In this case, let the law deal with it. I'll make sure they get everything that's coming to them."

"It sounds like you guys need to get ready to go out on stage," I said. The audience was gearing up again, albeit a bit more subdued now.

"Are you up to joining them?" Levi asked.

I blinked in surprise, then winced when it hurt.

My face would probably be a mess of bruises for a week or two. Thank God for makeup.

"I'm not sure the audience wants me out there." I sure as hell didn't want to be the target of things being thrown at me, whether they were bottles or insults. As it was, videos of me being struck in the face were undoubtedly going viral already.

The press were going to love every minute of this.

Fuck.

"A few assholes didn't," he agreed. "But me and the boys want you out there. And so does the majority of the audience. It's your choice, but if I were you I would show them you're not going to let a few dickheads hold you back. You haven't let them stop you yet, have you?"

"For the record," I said slowly, "offering me a challenge like that is totally unfair."

He grinned. "Good. Then get up and go out there and give them hell."

I sighed and let Asher and Zeke pull me to my feet. "Are you sure this is a good idea?"

"This is a great idea," Zeke said. "We'll be right beside you the whole time. If anyone tries anything, they'll have to go through us first."

"They might do that," I muttered. "I need to

change my shirt." Mine was covered in my blood. I ran a hand over the side of my hair. I would need to rinse that as well. Some of it was matted together.

"I need a shirt," Asher said. His was also covered in my blood.

"Do you?" Zeke asked him. "Do you really?" He managed to grin.

Asher grinned back. "Technically, no, but it wouldn't be fair to the other men in the audience to have my body on display like that. Just think how busy the ambos would be with fainting women."

"You have a point," Zeke said. "We wouldn't want anyone getting hurt because of your hotness."

We both gave Asher long, heated looks. Personally, I wouldn't mind seeing him play all shirtless and sweaty. People would probably pay good money to see that. And he would be worth every dollar.

Penn snorted.

"Send someone down to get a couple of band tees from the merch stand," Levi said to one of the festival volunteers. They nodded and turned to run off.

Only when they were out of sight, did Levi swear under his breath. "I should have specified Wolf Venom T-shirts. Hopefully they'll figure it out."

I laughed softly and winced. Singing with a

bandage on my cheek was going to be interesting, to say the least. I hoped this wasn't a bad omen for the rest of the tour.

In the back of my mind, I hoped even more that this had nothing to do with Zeke's family, somehow causing trouble this far away from Sydney. If they got desperate, they might try anything. Including injuring me to cause trouble for Zeke. Or to serve as a warning for us all.

21

ABBIE

IN THE END I only sang one song with the guys before bowing out.

In spite of maybe but probably not having a concussion, my head was still spinning and I needed to hunt down something for the pain.

At least Asher looked cute in a bright purple Wolf Venom T-shirt. Mine was an interesting shade of green.

The audience was much nicer the second time around too. They gave me a resounding applause when I stepped back out on the stage, and clapped when I left.

I found the first aid station easily enough. After they made a fuss and checked my already bruised face, they gave me some pills for the pain. I snagged a water bottle and flopped down in a camp chair backstage.

From here, I could sit back and enjoy watching the guys perform. They and the audience were having the time of their lives now. Considering all the drama, that was just as well. They came so close to missing out entirely. That would have been a shame for everyone.

Levi grabbed up another camp chair and sat down beside me. "Are you sure you're okay?" he asked over the music. "I can have someone drive you to your hotel if you want?"

"I'm fine." I took a swig of water and swallowed the second pain pill. "It's mostly my ego that's bruised. I'm used to people throwing accusations, but not cans. I don't know which is worse."

"Neither is okay." He still looked furious it happened at all. "I want to apologise. I should have liaised with the organisers better. What happened out there was completely preventable. No one— *No one* should step on that stage with any risk to their personal safety."

"Every time we step out there, we're risking something," I said with a shrug. "We all have bad days."

"In theory." He sucked in a breath and visibly

forced himself to relax. He turned toward the stage and took a few moments.

Without looking back at me, he said, "I don't think I've ever heard these guys have a bad day. Not on stage anyway. I heard about Jonah."

He didn't even change his tone before he added that last bit. Because of that, it took a moment for his words to sink in.

"Oh?" I asked slowly. How much did he know? My heart started to race like crazy. Was I about to get in a shit load of trouble?

He turned to give me a look like he was suppressing an eye roll at me for trying to play dumb. "He waved a gun at you and Zeke and ended up in a cardboard box."

"Ah." Apparently he knew everything. Perhaps that shouldn't surprise me, but it did. "How did you—"

"Jackson told me." He jerked his head in the general direction of the band's manager, who stood a few metres away, talking on his phone. "Nothing goes on within my label that I don't hear about sooner or later."

"So... you know there are similarities between that and what happened to Vance," I said. Sweat sprang up on my palms. "I had nothing to do with either of them."

If he didn't believe me, I was screwed. A sliver of panic wormed its way into my mind. Had he sat with me to tell me he was breaking my contract? Or calling the police? Or—

To my relief, he said, "I know you didn't." He crossed his legs at his knees. "You need to be careful. If someone is targeting you, we don't know if or when they might escalate."

I sat around the chair. "You think they might come after me?" I hadn't thought of that. I'd assumed they were trying to scare me. I hadn't considered I might be the target of a killer. Now I thought about it, I wished I hadn't.

"I would suggest that a person who leaves heads in cardboard boxes is probably not entirely sane," he said. "That being the case, you don't know when and where they might become more unhinged. Jackson said the guys have been making sure you're not left alone. I think it would be a good idea to keep doing that until we figure out who's behind this."

"Yeah, I guess so," I agreed reluctantly. I didn't want to be a burden to anyone, but the guys didn't seem to mind acting as my bodyguards. They all looked good doing it.

"I know you're an independent woman." He must have guessed at the reason for my reluctance. "But your safety is important to me. To the boys too, from what I've seen." He gave me a knowing look.

Yeah, I wasn't even slightly surprised he knew about that too.

"Is that a problem?" I asked. Some bosses didn't like their employees getting involved with each other, but this was a different situation to working in an office. The average label didn't have much say over their acts' personal lives. That didn't mean he didn't have an opinion.

"Not at all," he said lightly. "As long as it doesn't create drama. I like my label drama free."

"Good idea," I said dryly. I wished Onyx Riot had the same philosophy.

"Of course it is." He smiled smugly. "I'm happy to take credit for it."

I laughed. "You have plenty of good ideas you can take credit for. Like signing the boys." My gaze went back to them just as Channing began a saxophone solo.

"That's certainly one of my better ideas," Levi agreed. "Jackson tells me—"

Whatever he was going to say was interrupted by a loud voice speaking behind us.

"Of course Abbie will want to talk to me, we're old friends," Poppy Newton was saying.

I groaned.

"Fuck," Levi growled. He pushed himself up from the chair and he and Jackson both stepped towards the journalist.

"Who let her in here?" Jackson demanded.

"You took the words right out of my mouth," Levi said. "Security—"

Poppy smiled ingratiatingly at them both. "I won't take long. I just thought Abbie would like to address what happened on stage earlier."

"Are you following me?" I narrowed my eyes at her. "Shouldn't you be in Sydney annoying people?"

She clicked her tongue. "Don't be like that."

If there was a more annoying phrase, I couldn't think of it. I could be however I wanted to be. Right now that was pissed off.

"Someone threw something at me and got arrested. I'm fine. The end." I shrugged.

"You also got booed and had accusations thrown at you," she said smoothly. "Would you like to comment on those accusations?"

"No she wouldn't," Jackson snapped. "One of those is ancient history and the other is an ongoing police investigation. They've already ruled out her involvement, as you would be well aware if you've done your homework. Now, I suggest you leave before security removes you by force."

"Now," Levi added, if Jackson's words didn't have enough impact on the woman.

Poppy smiled over at me sweetly. "Which of these men are you sleeping with?"

If she thought she would take me by surprise, she was mistaken.

I laughed.

"Neither of them." I knew she was also referring to the band, but my answer was technically correct. Levi and Jackson were both attractive guys, but my hands were full enough as it was. Besides, neither had shown that kind of interest in me. They were both more like big brothers than potential lovers.

I thought about asking who she seduced to get in here in the first place, but I decided not to lower myself to her level. Let her deal in sleaze, I would get on with my life.

A couple of security people stepped to either side of her and one gestured toward the doorway. "This way please."

"Until next time," she said over her shoulder before she was herded away.

Jackson scrubbed his face with his hand. "That

woman is a fucking menace. Her and people like her. And people who read the shit she prints."

"She is a fucking vulture," Levi agreed. "The organisers are going to need to lift their game for next year if any of my bands are going to take part. No one should be coming backstage to harass any of the acts." He pulled a cigarette out of his pocket that looked like more than tobacco. "Excuse me, I need a smoke after all that."

He held out the joint towards me. "Do you want to join me?"

"No thank you." I waved a hand in refusal. "I've never been much of a fan. I'll have a few drinks later on, when the guys are finished playing." And if I was lucky, a few orgasms as well. Both of those things would go a long way to relieving my tension.

"Jax, keep an eye on her." Levi nodded towards me, then headed outside, in the opposite direction from which security took Poppy.

Jackson nodded and sat in the camp chair Levi had vacated.

"Jax?" I hadn't heard anyone call him that before.

He shrugged. "Levi and I go way back. He's the only one who gets away with calling me that."

I raised my hands in surrender. "I wasn't going to do it. I think it's cute he has a nickname for you.

People who've known me for a long time call me Abs." Ironic since now I seemed to be surrounded by guys with lots of abs.

"I'm sure they do," Jackson said. He looked like he had something else to say, but was trying to figure out how to approach the subject.

Finally, he said, "Tully told me what happened in Melbourne." He looked towards the floor, then back at me. "I'd like you to know you can come to me and tell me these things too. At some point, somebody is going to ask a question about something I don't know anything about. I need to know what's going on so I'm not caught off guard."

"Like Poppy Newton?" I asked.

"Exactly," he said. "I understand it's a difficult thing to talk about."

"Yeah, it is." How would I even start that conversation? Hey, Jackson, we found another head. Don't worry, we dealt with it with the help of Asher's sister. It's all good now.

I had a feeling he was suggesting I say just that.

"This doesn't bother you?" I asked. "I mean..." What did I mean? "People around me keep turning up dead. That's got to be disconcerting." I told him what Levi said about the killer possibly coming after me.

"It's a scary as fuck," he agreed. "That's why we're all keeping an eye on you and each other. We only get through this if we work together. Okay?"

I felt like he was telling me off, but he was right. If someone was after me, then I needed to trust the people who were trying to keep me safe. Likewise, they needed to trust me to keep them safe. I might not have big muscles, but I could punch and kick if I had to.

Plus I knew which way to point a gun now. That might come in useful someday.

"I'm sorry I didn't come to you and tell you," I said. "The next time I find a head..." I groaned. "What am I saying? I hope there *isn't* a next time. They might be finished making whatever point it was they were trying to make. Or maybe they got all that murder out of their system."

A girl could hope, right?

"I hope there isn't a next time too," Jackson said. "But we can't make any assumptions. We shouldn't relax until they catch whoever is doing this."

He rubbed his hands over his face. Managing a band and me was enough work without this thrown in on top of it. This must all be above his pay grade.

Hell, it was above mine.

"That could be hard when the police only know about Vance," I said.

"That's true," he said, "but his murder should give them enough clues to figure out who did it. Unless..."

"Unless what?" I didn't like the sound of that.

"Unless they're a professional," he finished.

"You mean hired by Zeke's family?" I suggested. "Zeke already ruled out Reuben's involvement, since Jonah worked for him."

"There's also Asher's family," he said.

"His sister helped us," I argued. Why would Asher's family come after me anyway? Unless this wasn't about me. If that was the case, then what was it about?

"That doesn't mean she isn't involved. Or that Dane isn't. I'm not necessarily saying they are, just that we can't rule out anything right now. With any luck, we won't see anything from them ever again."

"You don't believe that?" I asked.

He hesitated for a moment, then shook his head. "No, I don't. Just be careful and if you see anything weird, tell me. Okay?"

"Okay," I agreed. If I wasn't on edge before, I sure as fuck was now.

22

ASHER

"Is there a chance your family is involved with whoever is killing those people?" Abbie asked.

"Did Poppy Newton really turn up backstage?" I asked at the same time.

We both snort-laughed.

"You go first." I sat back in my seat and crossed my arms over my chest. It was going to be a long bus drive back to Brisbane, for the flight over to Perth. We might as well get comfortable.

"Jackson suggested the possibility of a professional leaving those... gifts," she said. "Zeke said it wasn't his family. I'm wondering if it might be yours. I don't know why they might come after me, but I don't know them like you do."

I scratched my forehead. "Me either. Dane and

Rose like you. I can't think of anyone else who might be involved, unless they're trying to fuck with Zeke. Who the fuck knows why these people do what they do?"

"Not me, that's for sure." She sighed. "I don't suppose there's any chance I pissed off the Bell family somehow?"

"Shit like this is definitely their style," I agreed. "I can't see it though. Hunter and Parker might have put Lila up to getting herself and her family involved, but I doubt it. They wouldn't risk pissing off Reuben by killing Jonah or going behind his back. If the family went after the Brantleys, they would go after Reuben, not hang around on the fringes trying to annoy Zeke. My money is on someone who isn't a professional. It's too sloppy for that."

"Sloppy?" she echoed.

"Yeah." I shrugged. "Anyone could have found them. Vance wasn't anywhere near the others. It's inconsistent. Not that I'm a detective or anything. I've just watched them on TV a few times."

She shook her head and smiled. "I'm sure that makes you an expert."

"Absolutely," I agreed. "In that case, I'm an expert on a shit load of things. Especially sex."

"Is that your way of telling me you watch a lot of porn?" She raised a perfectly shaped eyebrow at me.

"I wouldn't say a lot," I replied. Enough, but not recently. Why watch it when you can be doing it instead?

"You didn't answer my question about Poppy. How did she get backstage?"

"I have no idea." She stopped and frowned in thought. "Maybe she's the one doing it."

It took me a moment to realise what she was getting at. "You think she might be the one leaving those *gifts?*"

"She turned up here, a long way from home," Abbie said. "For all I know, she's getting paid to stalk me." She sighed out her nose. "I don't know, maybe I'm paranoid."

I hoped so, at least where Poppy Newton was concerned. If she was involved, then she wasn't working alone. She wasn't big enough to wrestle Jonah or Vance, much less cut their heads off. The killer had to be a man, or be working with a man.

I didn't tell her any of this; she was freaked out enough as it was.

"I think Poppy is out for money," I said slowly. "She might go a long way to get a story, but killing is extreme. Her career would be over if she was caught."

"Not just her career," Abbie said. "What if she was trying to pin it on me and get the scoop on it? Breaking a story like that would *make* her career."

"If that's the case, then I hope she gets the mental health care she clearly needs," I said. "Because that would be all kinds of fucked up."

"It really would," she agreed. "I suppose talking about it isn't going to get us anywhere, is it?"

"It's better than keeping your thoughts bottled up," I said. "I get you're scared."

I slipped an arm over her shoulders and pulled her to me as best I could with the seatbelts getting in the way. "I wish I knew who was doing this so I could end them."

She leaned her head against my chest. "You mean that literally? You would personally kill them?"

I couldn't tell if she was scared or turned on by that idea. Hopefully turned on.

"If I have to," I admitted. "There's nothing I wouldn't do to keep you safe and happy. There's nothing any of us wouldn't do." I waved a hand around the bus and the guys nodded. Most of them.

"I have a limit or two," Penn said.

"What a shock," Abbie said sarcastically. She

waved a hand at him before he could retort. "I don't expect you to do anything because of me. Any of you. I certainly don't expect you to do anything illegal."

"You might not expect it, but that doesn't mean it wouldn't happen." I grinned. We all lived our professional lives totally above board, but our personal lives toed the line once in a while.

She shook her head at me. "I don't want you to get arrested doing anything to keep me safe."

"I won't," I said. "They'd have to catch me first. I'm sure you noticed, some of us have families who know exactly how to get us out of the shit before things get too far. "

"But at what price?" she asked. "Zeke going back to his family? You going back to yours?"

"Whatever the price has to be," I said firmly. "We're not losing you. Whatever happens, we'll deal with it. Together. Okay?"

She sighed. "Okay. I just… I hope you don't regret anything. That's all. I feel like I've turned all of your lives upside down."

Penn turned his face, but for once kept his mouth shut.

"Yes, you have," I told her. "In the best way possible. Firstly, we got to meet you, and you are incredibly special. Secondly, Zeke and I would be best buddies until the end of time if you hadn't helped us to open our eyes to each other."

I looked across the aisle at Zeke and smiled at him. I could hardly believe we made that step. I'd have to write a song about how I felt, because I couldn't put it into words or even coherent thought. Everything changed and it was all for the better.

He smiled back. "What Asher said. Being best buddies wouldn't be so bad, but I like this more." He reached across the aisle to put his hand over mine.

"Me too," I said.

Channing and Landon gave a shout. I jumped and I looked back over my shoulder. They were both leaning over, looking out the window.

I sat forward and tried to figure out what they were looking at.

"Smartass." Beside us, in a bright red Porsche, with the top all the way down, was Levi Jones. He wore a leather jacket and sunglasses and probably looked cooler than I did right now. Honestly, he looked cooler than any of us did right now.

He waved over at us and revved the engine. He had the biggest smile on his face.

"Is he trying to race the bus?" Abbie asked with a laugh.

"It certainly looks like it." As bosses went, Levi was a long way from the suit wearing, stick up the ass kind, that was for sure. We all smelled weed on him more than once, and apparently now he wanted us to take part in an illegal race on the highway.

The man was a fucking legend. He probably had a woman with her face in his lap as well, because why not? If anyone could get away with it, it would be him.

The bus driver revved the engine in response, but the old girl wasn't up to going much faster than she already was. She was certainly not going to contend with a Porsche, no matter how much we wished it would.

"He totally makes the rest of us make sense, doesn't he?" I asked. "I mean, he's obviously insane and so are we."

Tully, Landon and Channing were all standing up and waving their arms out the window at Levi. It was like being on the school bus back in high school or something.

Abbie shook her head. "Insane might just be the right word, yes. At least everyone is having a good time doing it."

I looked from the window to her. She'd taken the bandage off her face already, revealing a hell of a bruise. The mark from the can was starting to heal. I didn't think it would leave a scar.

At this point, I didn't know who was luckier, her or the idiot who threw the can. If she was badly hurt, I would have hunted him down and badly hurt *him*.

What sort of prick throws things at someone on stage, especially a woman?

If you want to throw things, take up a sport, or at least throw things at people who deserve it. Like that Poppy Newton bitch. I wished I was there backstage when she appeared. I would have given her a one way ticket out of the venue, on the end of my foot.

"Awww," the other guys groaned in disappointment.

Levi accelerated and pulled his Porsche away from the bus. In a minute or two, he was completely out of sight.

Ironically, he'd likely only get back to Brisbane a couple of minutes before us, but he had to do it in style.

"I'm starting to think you guys are just overgrown boys," Abbie said.

I raised my eyebrows at her. "Oh? You hadn't realised that already?" A slow grin crept onto my face. "I thought that was what you liked about us." I pouted playfully.

"It is," she said. "You guys know how to have fun, no matter what you do. I hope you never stop doing that."

"If we do, you have my permission to smack my ass and remind me to keep having fun," I said. "Actually, you can smack my ass anytime." I looked over to Zeke. "That goes for you too."

"I might just take you up on that." He gave me a speculative look and a slight eyebrow wiggle. Fuck, he was so hot, that look made my cock hard.

Of course, now my mind was racing in about fifty different directions, all of them to do with being sweaty and naked with Zeke and Abbie.

When she was lying on the ground with blood on her face, I heard Tully mention plans for a date in Perth.

I knew exactly what that meant and I was all for it, but I wondered how that would change our dynamic.

Hopefully for the better. I was here for it.

23

ABBIE

"WE'VE GOT to go to Gate Twelve," Zeke said.

We arrived at the airport just in time to catch our flight to Adelaide.

A lot of acts, especially international ones, never made it to South Australia, or Western Australia.

Personally, Perth and Adelaide were two of my favourite places to perform. Maybe because concert-goers appreciated actually getting to see someone for a change.

With any luck, they'd build a large venue in Canberra, so we could perform there as well. The capital of Australia missed out on a lot of acts, but there wasn't anywhere big enough for an act like Wolf Venom.

What they had was fine for someone like me, but

the guys needed a bigger capacity. Otherwise they'd play every night for a year to fit everyone in.

"For once, I'm glad to have interviewers waiting for us," Landon said. "It's a long fucking drive from Brisbane to Adelaide. We've done it a few times before."

Honestly, under any other circumstances, I would have travelled with the cars and vans, but the guys weren't going to let me out of their sight. When they had to fly, so did I.

Was I arguing with that? Hell no.

"At least we don't get to miss the joy of driving over the Nullarbor plain from Adelaide to Perth," Asher said with a grimace. "Kilometre after kilometre of absolutely nothing."

"It's a good chance to catch up on naps," Channing said.

"You mean it's a good chance for us to listen to you snore for hours on end," Penn told him.

Channing grinned. "It doesn't bother me."

Penn snorted. "Of course it wouldn't? You're asleep at the time, dumbass."

In spite of his words, a hint of a smile on the corners of his mouth showed he was teasing.

If he wasn't, Channing wouldn't give a crap

anyway. He knew Penn well enough not to take anything he said too personally.

I shook my head and smiled as they bickered with each other. They wouldn't be them without razzing each other every chance they got.

Zeke slipped his hand into mine. That earned us some curious and even jealous looks from people who passed us by and recognised the guys.

If they only knew the half of it.

"I haven't had a chance to talk to you properly since the festival," he said. "I've been trying to think what to say."

He paused for a moment, looking regretful and angry. "I should have been on stage with you. Or closer than I was before any fucking cans started to fly. I'm pissed off at myself. I screwed up. I'm sorry for letting you down."

I looked up at him as we walked. "Zeke Brantley, none of that was in any way your fault. You're not my babysitter, or my bodyguard, and you can't stand right next to me on stage every time I step out there, in case something happens." I wouldn't put it past him to try.

"If you're going to do that, I might as well not step out there at all. Or I'll have the staff erect a Perspex shield so I can stand behind that while I perform." That wouldn't be weird *at all*. Yeah, fuck that.

"That might be a good idea." He looked thoughtful.

I poked him in the chest. "I'm not performing behind a wall. I'd prefer not to perform at all. I could take a flight back to Sydney right now." I turned and took half a step in the opposite direction.

He pulled me back to his side and tucked me firmly against his hip. "You're not going back without me, and I'm under contract so I can't go back. You're coming with me if I have to tie you up and carry you over my shoulder. Actually, that's a good idea."

He stopped walking and pretended to lower his shoulder to lift me up onto it.

I took a real step back. "Don't you fucking dare." I pointed at him with a finger of my spare hand, then shook it a few times under his nose.

"Fine, I won't, but don't pretend you're not coming with us." He tugged me towards the gate.

"Of course I'm coming with you," I said. "But stop blaming yourself for what happened. It's not your fault. It's the fault of a handful of assholes who will probably be banned from events like that for life."

They wouldn't get any sympathy from me. Whatever they got, they deserved it.

"Whether or not it's my fault, I'm gonna keep being salty about it for a while," he said.

"Zeke is good at taking things to heart," Asher said. "It's one of the things we love about him. He's broody and intense, and protective. And ready to belt the shit out of anyone who crosses us."

"I've noticed that about him." I smiled up at Zeke. "It's definitely part of his charm."

"Only a small part," Zeke said modestly. He gave us both a lopsided smile.

"Yeah, that's what Zeke needs," Penn said sarcastically. "A bigger motherfucking ego. You know they can't take the top of the plane off to fit your head in it if it gets any bigger."

Zeke grinned. "If it can fit your ego, it can fit mine."

Penn groaned while the rest of us laughed.

Asher patted him on the shoulder. "You walked right into that, Penny."

"Fuck off," Penn told him. Again, he looked like he was trying hard not to smile.

I wondered if his face would crack if he actually did. It might, or he might look even more attractive than when he scowled. Would I ever get to find out? I hoped so.

"We probably need a bigger plane for all of our egos," Tully said. "They're pretty healthy."

No one argued with that.

We stopped at Gate Twelve as they started to board everyone onto the plane.

The attendant paid more attention to our boarding passes than they did to any of us. Hundreds and hundreds of people walked past them every day. Plenty of them more famous than any of us.

At least, more famous than me.

We were waved through the bridge and onto the plane. Predictably, the guys herded me into the middle seat of the side with three seats. Asher sat on the window and Zeke sat on the aisle. Channing and Landon sat behind us and Tully and Penn sat in front.

"You know they're going to want to interview you too, right?" Zeke asked.

"What?" I blinked at him. "Jackson said they wanted to interview you guys."

He shrugged one shoulder. "They're still going to want to talk to you."

"And you're telling me this now because the door

to the plane closed and I can't get up and run away?"
I raised one eyebrow at him.

He grinned. "Do I seem that devious to you?"

I raised the other eyebrow at him.

"Ouch, you wound me, woman." He pressed a
hand to his chest over his heart.

"I'm just getting started," I growled playfully.

"I'm sure you are." He lowered his hand. "For the
record, I thought of it as we sat down. You would
have come to the same conclusion in a hot minute.
We're touring together and people are curious about
you after all the things they've heard. Without doubt
they'll want to ask about the festival. If they didn't
know who you were before, they will now. Who
wouldn't be interested in someone who tried to
catch a can with their face?"

While he smiled, I socked him in the chest.

"If I tried to catch it, I would have done a better
job of it than that," I told him. "Even with my face."

I lightly touched my cheek. It only hurt a little bit
now. The concealer I applied this morning covered
the bruising so no one would know it was there,
even if they looked close. Keeping myself from
flinching at anything heading toward my face, that
instinct would last a while longer.

"As much as I would like to see you catch a can

with your face, I won't suggest we try that," he said. "Unless you want to introduce it as part of your act. In which case—"

I turned to Asher. "Do you think they would let us throw him out at a hundred thousand feet?"

Asher looked thoughtful, but his blue eyes shone with mischief. "I don't know, we could ask. Do we want the parachute included in this special offer or just a shove?"

"Ha fucking ha," Zeke said sarcastically. "Neither of you would push me out of a plane. You both love me too much." He gave us both an intense look that spoke volumes about the way he felt.

"We certainly wouldn't push you out of a plane," I agreed. I was going to add something nice, maybe even admit that I did love him.

Asher spoke before I could.

"No, we wouldn't, because if they opened the door it would depressurise the plane and we would all die."

"At least I would take you with me," Zeke said.

"How about you fucking don't," Penn said over his shoulder. "I'm too young and hot to die." And he said Zeke had an ego. His was certainly equally robust. With good reason, admittedly.

"Yes you are," Asher told him. "So am I."

"We all are," Landon called out from behind us.

The plane jolted and started to taxi towards the runway.

A little flutter of nerves passed through me. Partly at the prospect of another city and more concerts, partly at the idea of interviews. And partly at the idea of getting closer to Perth and my date with Tully. Added to that the idea of talking about the festival and the worry of whoever was stalking me might be following right behind us.

The list of reasons to have nerves seem to get longer and longer every day.

To think, a few weeks ago the only thing I was worried about was going on tour and getting my career back on track. Now everything seemed so much more complicated. Some things, like my growing relationships with the guys, were amazing, but the constant need to look over my shoulder sucked hairy donkey balls.

Would I have embarked on this journey if I'd known what I was getting myself into?

I thought about that for a moment and realised the answer was easy. It was a resounding yes, with a nice long chorus and an even longer bridge. Even with the shadow of a killer hanging over us, I wouldn't have missed any of this for the world.

Like Tully said, we were always meant to find each other. I believed that with my whole heart. One way or another, we would have met up and connected.

I didn't know why we were set on such a difficult path, but we would travel it together and we would come out the other end stronger than ever.

In the back of my mind was the lingering thought that we had to survive it all first. When I looked to my left and my right, in front of me and behind, I was surrounded by six muscular, intelligent, protective guys. I couldn't be safer.

I may not sing behind a wall, but I was surrounded by one. A big, badass wall of smoking hot muscle. If the universe put me through all that shit so I could end up here with them, then maybe the universe was looking out for me after all.

I really was one lucky fucking girl. Wasn't I?

24

ABBIE

THE PLANE LEVELLED off and the *fasten seatbelt* light went out. Because I didn't want to tempt fate to fuck with me again, I left mine on just in case. The guys all unclicked theirs and reclined their seats as far as they would go.

Except for Asher. He looked over at me with a smile on his face.

"What?" I knew that look and I should probably know better than to ask.

He leaned over closer to me and whispered in my ear. "Have you joined the mile high club?"

Heat crept up my neck and onto my face that was less a blush than a pulse of excitement.

"No," I said. "Have you?" Wait, did I really want an

answer to that? I didn't care about their past sex lives, but I didn't necessarily need specifics.

Instead of answering, he asked another question. "Do you want to?" He put a hand on the top of my thigh.

I looked around. "I don't know. Would we get in trouble?" They couldn't throw us off the plane, but they could turn it around and leave us back in Brisbane.

He grinned. "Nah, it'll be fine. Come on."

I glanced back at Zeke.

He also grinned. "Go on, have fun. There's not enough room in there for three anyway."

I leaned over to kiss him lightly on the mouth. "You're the best."

"Fuck yeah I am." He slipped on the headphones provided by the airline and started to groove to whatever music was playing through the system. Probably Wolf Venom.

I undid my seatbelt and followed Asher through the aisle of the plane, to the tiny toilet. I didn't dare to look back over my shoulder to see if anyone was watching us. If there was, there would be no doubt as to what we were up to.

It crossed my mind that someone might take a photo and that would be the next thing about me to go viral, but I couldn't bring myself to give a shit anymore. It might be a welcome distraction from people talking about throwing cans, and stray heads.

"This is definitely a tight fit." Asher pressed me back against the sink and slid his hands up my shirt and across my stomach.

"Yeah, they really could make these a bit more spacious," I said. "With room for a shower and a bath. Maybe a king-size bed."

He chuckled. "I'll be sure to insist on a private jet and not a commercial flight next time."

"You do that." I ran my hands over the front of his pants and felt his cock harden under my touch.

He had more influence with the label than I did. On the other hand, sure Levi Jones drove a Porsche, but he wasn't made of money. Not yet.

I undid the front of his pants and worked them down far enough to free his erection. I curled my fingers around his cock and stroked him a few times.

"Mmmm." He pushed himself deeper into my hand and rucked up my skirt. He pulled the front of my panties aside and slid the tips of a couple of fingers down my seam and over my clit. His other hand went down my leg until he gripped my thigh and pulled up my knee to open me out to him.

We worked each other for a couple of minutes

until we were both breathless and I was as wet as fuck.

"I need you inside me," I whispered. Between his touch and the vibration of the plane, I was feeling wobbly at the knees. I leaned back between the sink and what little wall there was and let him hold me in place while he positioned his cock outside my pussy.

"Abbie," he said softly. "Fuck, you are amazing." With almost teasing slowness, he slid his full length into me.

I groaned in pleasure at how full he made me feel. I forgot the close surroundings and lost myself in the moment.

While his hands were busy holding me in place, I reached up with one of mine to massage my own nipple through the fabric of my shirt and bra. Then the other one.

"That is fucking hot," he said. "Would you rub your clit for me?"

His words were almost enough to make me come on the spot, but I slipped my hand down between my legs and started to trace slow circles around my clit.

"That's my girl," he whispered. He thrust in and out of me slowly, his stomach nudging my hand every time he drove in deep.

"This was a good idea of yours," I said.

"Hell yeah, I agree." He was already panting and his voice was ragged.

I wanted to tell him I loved him, but the time wasn't right. I didn't know why but it wasn't. When the time came, I'd shout it from the rooftops.

Instead, I said, "I'm going to come."

"Mmm, please do. I'll be right behind you." He thrust a little harder.

"How about you come at the same time as me?" My breath was just as ragged.

"Like, on the count of three?" He grinned.

"I don't think I'm that disciplined," I said breathlessly. "That might be something we can work on."

"Absolutely." He looked at me through half closed eyes. "I want to teach you to come on command. That will be fun when you're out on the stage.

I started to laugh, but it came out as a moan.

"Don't you dare." That would be…interesting. If no one knew it was happening, it could be fun. I put that into the 'maybe' pile to think about later.

I closed my eyes and rubbed myself a little harder, while I bucked my hips in unison to him. I gripped his upper arm with my spare hand and dug my nails into his skin as I came.

He came at the same time, thrusting harder and breathing heavily.

Holy shit, there was something particularly hot about hearing someone orgasm while you're in the throes of one yourself. It made me come again, just as I was coming down from the first one. The second one was deeper, more intense and possibly involved fireworks, rainbows and a meteor shower or two.

When I came down fully, I was a panting, weak kneed mess of deep satisfaction and a whole lot of wet, sticky cum.

"Oh yeah." Asher leaned his head against the wall for a minute or two before he slid out of me and let my leg back down. "Welcome to the club, baby."

"You too," I said, since he hadn't answered the question about it earlier.

He smiled and kissed my mouth, brushing his tongue over my lips and teeth.

I kissed him back, then reluctantly pulled back and said, "I need to get cleaned up."

That began a couple of minutes of awkward shuffling around the tiny space, but we finally got sorted out and unlocked the door.

I hoped to sneak out without anyone paying

much attention to us, but the minute we stepped out the door, the plane erupted into applause.

I clapped a hand over my face, which was burning hot and probably fire engine red, and hurried back to slip into my seat.

I didn't even peek out from between my fingers to see if anyone was videoing us. They probably were. Wasn't that the point of phones? To video people doing things and sharing it with the world later? People could get away with anything these days. That was both a blessing and a curse.

Oh well, I would deal with it if it went viral. I had, after all, made my bed by going in there with him in the first place.

Asher, being Asher, grinned and raised his hands to accept every piece of attention. He slipped back into his seat looking like the cat that got the cream.

People definitely took photos and videos of him doing his walk of fame. It wouldn't do his reputation any harm.

I shook my head and resisted the urge to grab a blanket and put it over my face for the rest of the flight. I should have realised we'd be noticed, and maybe even overheard. I wished I dared to own it the way he did. Maybe someday.

"That was some wild turbulence." Zeke looked

happy Asher and I got to have that time alone. Giving his blessing and being okay with it could have been very different things.

Lucky for me, both of them were so accepting and open. There didn't seem to be a drop of jealousy between them. Not even when it came to the other guys. What did I fucking do to deserve to even meet these beautiful boys? Whatever it was, it must have been really good.

Really, really good.

I frowned at Zeke. "There wasn't—" I realised he was teasing. I slapped him lightly on the chest. "You're such a brat."

He laughed. "I'm sorry, I couldn't resist."

"You don't sound sorry at all." I looked at him through narrowed, but playful eyes.

He just went on grinning and looked over the top of the chairs. "Looks like you came just in time for lunch. That was lucky. There would be nothing worse than going hungry while getting your fill."

I decided to ignore his puns. "Good, I'm hungry." There was nothing like sex to work up an appetite. I couldn't argue with his turn of phrase either. I did get my fill. Asher had an impressively thick cock.

"Me too," Zeke said. "And this is an almost three-hour flight. There's plenty of time for an extra snack later, if you're feeling up to it."

"It wouldn't go unnoticed if I went in there with two different guys on the same flight," I remarked.

"That's true," he agreed. "If people are going to talk, we might as well give them something interesting to talk about."

"Maybe," I said slowly.

Who was it that said fame is a bitch? If we were absolute nobodies, no one would care what we got up to.

No, I wasn't that naïve. Either way, it would end up on social media and people would talk. I could imagine the names I'd get called, whereas the guys would be thought of as heroes.

Fucking double standard.

"Let's eat first and think about the rest of it later." I wasn't going to lie, the idea of screwing Zeke on board the plane was very appealing, even without the king-sized bed.

Okay, the idea of fucking him anywhere was hot. I couldn't get enough of him or Asher. I was looking forward to figuring out a few things with Tully too. And the other three guys.

Was I turning into some kind of sex fiend or

something? I was thinking about it a lot more than I ever had before. The more I got, the more I wanted.

I was one hundred percent here for every bit of it.

In the back of my mind, I was scared about what the future would hold. Not just worrying about killers and people throwing cans, but what would happen when the tour was over? Would we be forced to go our separate ways? Would the guys all forget about me and move on to other people?

The idea was like a wrench around my heart, twisting it almost to breaking point.

I didn't want to live my life separately from the guys and I didn't want to move on with anyone else. Somehow, I was going to have to find a way to broach the conversation with each of them. I needed to know what they wanted and what they needed.

I hoped to hell what they wanted and needed was me.

25

ABBIE

"That journalist was nicer than Poppy Newton," Tully remarked as we walked out of the studio together.

"That wouldn't be hard," I said dryly. He was right though. Xander Riley was much nicer than Poppy and a shit load more respectful. He wanted to talk to me, but he only asked about the can and if I was okay. He seemed genuinely concerned that someone would throw things at a performer on the stage.

He asked what my thoughts were on preventing future incidents like that.

All I could say was to suggest security remove any troublemakers as soon as they could, and provide lots of bins for empty cans. What else could

they do? They could ban cans, cups and bottles alto-
gether, but people would go thirsty and go home.

As much as I'd like to prevent anyone else from
getting hurt, greater measures would only ruin the
fun for those who were there to have a good time.

I told him that as well. The last thing I wanted to
do was rain on anyone's parade.

He nodded at that and turned his attention to the
guys, and I got to sit back and relax.

He didn't ask any hard-hitting questions, but it
was nice to listen to the guys answer the ones he did
ask. Mostly they were about their favourite songs,
the process of writing songs and any highlights of
the present tour or past tours.

There wasn't one question about anyone's
personal life or their sex life. If anyone videoed
Asher and me coming out of the plane toilet, it
wasn't mentioned.

So far, nothing surfaced. With any luck, it
wouldn't.

"Did Jackson give him a list of questions to ask?" I
walked between the guys as we headed to our hotel.
It was a nice day and only about ten minutes away.

Spending time being normal like this was a
refreshing change to the crazy pace we had the last
couple of weeks. And the crazy pace we would have

after the Perth concerts. Once we left Australia, it would be go, go, go for the next couple of months.

I was looking forward to it, but I'd also appreciate this downtime. I mean, any chance I got to be with the guys was a bonus as far as I was concerned.

"Probably," Asher said. "But Xavier doesn't deal in sleaze and bullshit anyway. His angle is the light, fluffy stuff. His job is to make us look good so we'll talk to him again. It's a mutually beneficial arrangement."

"That makes sense," I said. "I would be happy to talk to him again. That was much less stressful than I thought it would be." I wished all journalists were like him. Light and fluffy was something I could get behind all day every day.

Zeke hung an arm over my shoulders. "See, you have nothing to worry about. And if you did, we would have kicked his ass."

"I appreciate that," I said. "But I don't think that would have gone down very well."

"Not as well as you and I on that flight," he agreed.

I grinned. I still couldn't work out exactly how we'd managed that, but we had. We even got another round of applause afterwards. I might have even given a small bow to the plane full of people.

Honestly, a few of the women look at me like I was a hero. That was a refreshing change. I much preferred that to being treated like a slut.

"It's a shame we're driving over to Perth," Asher said.

Zeke hung an arm over his shoulders as well. "Luckily rest stops are a thing."

We were all smiling and laughing as we walked through the front doors into the hotel.

We managed to make it up to the sixth floor in the elevator without anyone fucking anyone else, and stepped out into the corridor that led to our rooms.

"Who brought the extra suitcase?" Asher asked.

"The what?" I looked questioningly at him, and then down the corridor.

Sure enough, a small suitcase with the handle slightly raised, was parked outside the door to the room I would share with Zeke, Asher and Tully.

I stopped mid-step. "Please tell me suitcases aren't the new cardboard box."

Zeke approached it carefully. "There's no tag on it, so it didn't come on the flight with us. It's possible one of the roadies left it here, thinking it was ours."

It certainly looked like one of the suitcases the tour staff travelled with, but they weren't any different to the average suitcase you could buy from just about anywhere.

"Is it ticking?" Asher asked.

"Not that I can hear," Zeke said. "We should take it in and have a look."

I didn't like that idea, but the alternative was worse. Mostly, that meant leaving it there for someone else to find.

"It's probably got someone's spare underwear inside." Asher pulled out his key card and unlocked the door.

Zeke picked up the case by its handle and carried it carefully inside. We all piled into the room before Asher closed the door behind us.

Zeke crouched beside the suitcase and, with a look of fierce concentration on his face, gripped the zip and wound it around so the case opened.

"That was what I was afraid of," he said.

"What?" I asked.

He opened it all the way.

My stomach turned at the sight of Poppy Newton staring back at me. Even dead, she seemed to be accusing me of something.

"Fucking hell."

Asher slipped an arm around me. "That must have come here via the rest of the tour luggage. So whoever did that stashed it with the rest of the equipment—"

"Or the killer is a part of the tour," I finished for him.

THANKS FOR READING! The story continues in book 3, Session.

ABOUT THE AUTHOR

Maggie Alabaster writes reverse harem and, paranormal, sci-fi and fantasy romance.

She lives in NSW, Australia with one spouse, two daughters, one dog, and countless birds.

Jo Bradley is her alternate personality. She writes contemporary romance.

Sign up for my newsletter! Sign Up!

Join my reader group! Join here!

Follow me on Bookbub! Click here to follow me!

Check out my website- www.maggiealabaster.com

ALSO BY MAGGIE ALABASTER

Saving Abbie

Book 1 Pitch

Book 2 Pound

Book 3 Session

Book 4 Muse

Book 5 Rhythm

Book 6 Encore

Ruthless Claws

Book 1 Ivory

Book 2 Crimson

Book 3 Elodie

Harmony's Magic

Book 1 Summoned by Fire

Book 2 Summoned by Fate

Book 3 Summoned by Desire

Shifter's Vault

Book 1 Discarded

Also by Maggie Alabaster and Erin Yoshikawa

Caught by the Tide

Book 1–Pursued by Shadows

Book 2 Pursued by Darkness

Book 3 Pursued by Monsters